Praise

"Kristine Scarrow writes about ordinary people trying to survive the unbearable. However, these stories are neither cautionary tales nor distant tragedies. Grounded in realism, the author doesn't neatly mend the broken, but offers the reader the more genuine experience of bearing witness to uncertain outcomes."

- Paula Jane Remlinger, author of
***This Hole Called January*, winner of the**
2020 Saskatchewan Book Award for Poetry

"Life weighs heavily on Kristine Scarrow's characters in these finely wrought stories of everyday life, stories that are intimate, close-up, and personal. As readers we bear witness to these characters' often heartbreaking struggles throughout which Scarrow's authorial lens remains one of deep compassion for the loneliness, longing, suffering, but also connection and love that ground our humanity."

- Jeanette Lynes, Bestselling Author of
The Paper Birds* and *The Apothecary's Garden

"There's a patience and emotional intelligence in Scarrow's writing, grounded in details of daily life, that make the characters true and recognizable. The word 'pathos' hardly seems sufficient to describe the impact of some of these stories. Her pallete includes some quite enjoyable humour, or at least a bit of bizzare irony when needed. A compelling book I read in one sitting."

- Bruce Rice, author of *Standstill:*
A Hopewell Earthworks Daybook and Other Essays

Copyright © Kristine Scarrow

For permission, please address Wild Skies Press.

Published 2026
Printed in Canada

ISBN Paperback: 978-1-997770-09-1
ISBN E-Book: 978-1-997770-10-7

Cover Design by Alexis Marie Chute
Interior Design by Alexis Marie Chute
Stock media: Pixabay

For information or bulk orders address:
Wild Skies Press
A division of Alexis Marie Productions Inc.
Edmonton, Alberta, Canada
info@alexismariechute.com
www.WildSkiesPress.com

Wild Skies Press is an independent literary publisher founded in 2021. Wild Skies refers to the Aurora Borealis—northern lights—in Alberta, where the press is located, situated on Treaty 6 Territory. Wild Skies Press publishes non-fiction, fiction, poetry, and hybrid genres with an emphasis on the creation of books by emerging and established authors.

www.WildSkiesPress.com

For my mom, who championed education
and learning for her children and instilled
in me my everlasting love affair with
reading, books, and libraries.

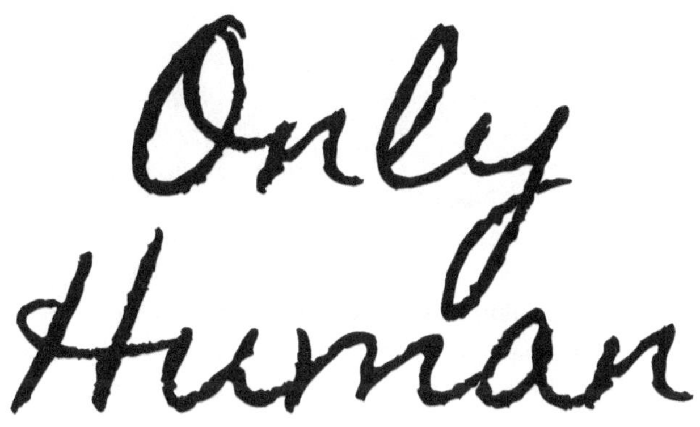

Only Human

Short Stories

Kristine Scarrow

The following short stories span the breadth of human experience—the highs and the lows. As the author does not shy from the rawness of her topic, telling these tales authentically and deeply, we must advise readers now of content that might be found upsetting by some.

These include mention of child death ("Sunny View" and "Crash"), illness and death ("In Sickness and in Health"), and child molestation ("The Game Isn't Fun Anymore").

Stories

Sunny View

Aida Phillips, a forty-three-year-old woman, an accountant by trade, long-limbed and lithe from years of competitive swimming, sat in her underwear on the cool marble floor of the main bathroom. Wads of tear-soaked toilet paper peppered the floor.

She studied her toes; overgrown jagged toenails painted in cherry red polish with ugly chips that looked like mini blood spatters. Unshaven, the hair on her legs was baby soft again as it grew past the stubble she was used to. Her bathrobe, tattered and worn and stained in too many places, hung limply from her slumped shoulders. She ran her hand under the thin, cotton nightgown she was wearing and placed it over her belly, hoping for the taut, firm roundness of life growing inside of her. Instead, her fingers sunk into pillowy soft folds of flesh, cushioning her palm. She wept.

Her body that had once carried life—housed it, nourished it, spoke to it, now felt monstrous: once again, there were no hormones in her blood this month indicating reproductive success. Her body was volatile, repelling. Like clockwork each month, she'd stare at the crimson clots, the lining of her womb as it shed itself, leaving her uterus barren and cavernous once again. Her body continued to betray her and malfunction—an added cross to bear.

There were more ways than one to be broken. Marvin, her husband of ten years, had grown tired of spending his time at home on the bathroom floor. He'd still check in on her, of course, but gone were the days when he'd crouch down on the shiny pearl-coloured floor and cup his sturdy frame around her. His touch used to quell her body's unrelenting shaking. Some days she'd even find herself settling into him and relaxing. There had been more hope back then—hope that life as they'd once known it would return in some manner with time. But so far, the only thing time had brought was more heartache.

Aida heard the door open. Marvin was home. A part of her wanted to stand and smooth her hair. Gather herself and meet him at the door, like a good wife. She cocked her head, hoping to hear his footsteps approach. The house remained eerily quiet. She imagined him seated on the couch, scrolling through his iPhone or staring out the living room window, through the sheer cream Hunter Douglas blinds she'd had custom designed when they'd moved into the house. The blinds could even be controlled by a remote, a luxury that still surprised her.

She imagined him staring out at 127, the newly renovated sprawling bungalow across the street. A new couple had moved in last month. The husband was short and mousy looking. Forgettable. He'd transferred from another city to work at the food lab at the university. She couldn't remember his name. The wife, equally petite, was a pretty thing. She could pass as a teenager, with her youthful smile and tiny stature. She was one of those young women who was perpetually happy. Anytime Aida saw her through the window, she was smiling, even if she was all alone. Aida hadn't met her yet.

At first it had intrigued her, how this woman could smile all the time. But soon, it irritated her. No one was that happy. Anyone that pleasant must be harbouring a dark secret of some sort. Her irritation grew to a seething burn when instead of parking in their attached garage as she normally would, the wife began parking in the driveway. One day, she proceeded to scoop out a baby car seat from the back of their BMW sedan. How had Aida never noticed that they had a child?

She felt a flame of heat in her gut every time she caught a glimpse of the baby. Moreover, Aida imagined Marvin standing at the blinds, stalker-like, staring at the pretty, young wife and fantasizing about her. Taking in her delicate features and her cheery disposition. She came across like a happy puppy, eager to please. Marvin would love a woman like that in his life. Someone ready to give, give, give.

Aida turned onto her hands and knees and rose to the vanity mirror. Her legs shook from the strain of standing. Her reflection in the bathroom mirror startled her. Ugly grey-violet rings framed her eyes. Her face had thinned further; her cheekbones stood out like sharp peaks on a once beautiful canvas. Aida took a deep breath and turned the doorknob to exit the bathroom. The hallway was an emotional landmine she needed to prepare for. They kept the bedroom doors closed, but she still felt her chest tighten every time she passed the last door on the left. She stepped gingerly through the hallway, the balls of her feet the only part touching the floor.

Late afternoon sunlight poured into the west facing picture window, only partially filtered by the blinds. Aida had to raise her hand to her brow to shield against the unexpected light. She expected to find Marvin standing at the window, but the room was empty, and no sound of his presence could be heard. Aida gazed around the living room and shivered.

What once was a handsome, sleek space now felt sparse and harsh. The iconic black Eames chair, the beige tufted-back couch, the cool walls painted in Stonington Gray. It had all been carefully curated for their "forever" house. Clean, straight lines that felt sturdy and sure. The clerk at the paint store had insisted that the room would not be too stark, but Aida felt it clinical, impersonal.

Aida heard the slamming of a car door. She approached the window. There she was, the neighbour woman, schlepping a jet-black baby stroller from the trunk of her car. The baby's car seat was also on the driveway, its back to her, so she couldn't see the child. She watched as the woman picked up the car seat, snapped it securely into place within the stroller frame and tucked a knitted blanket over the front.

The woman pranced down the driveway and onto the sidewalk. Aida craned her neck to watch her. She turned and now Aida could only see the back of her. Aida blinked and decided there was only one thing to do. She let her bathrobe fall to the floor, flung open the small closet in the front entry, threw on a long black coat and slipped her bare feet into her running shoes. They were scuffed and well-worn from earlier days of regular fitness.

When the brisk fall air hit her bare legs, Aida hesitated for just a second before pulling the wooden door behind her. Dry, brittle leaves swirled around her feet as she walked. Aida kept her gaze on the back of her neighbour, her bright pink windbreaker, black leggings, running shoes, and her perfectly coiffed copper ponytail that swung wildly with her strides.

Aida quickened her pace to close the gap between her and the stroller. The last thing she wanted was to lose them. This renewed purpose injected her with life. She watched intently as her neighbour turned out of sight. She had veered toward the park and playground that bordered the next street over from their crescent. Aida moved into a slow jog. A delivery truck blared its horn at her. She slowed briefly—unstartled—noting that she had stepped onto the street without looking, her eyes fixated on her neighbour ahead.

"Get outta the way, lady!" A bearded man in checkered flannel hollered from the driver's side window. Aida simply carried on.

When she reached the entrance to the park, Aida's heart hammered in her chest. There her neighbour was, comfortably perched on a park bench, bouncing the baby lightly in her lap. The last rays of sun illuminated the child's face and Aida could tell the child was bright-eyed and smiling, even from a distance.

Aida shuffled toward the park bench, careful not to startle the two of them. As she approached, her neighbour's head shifted toward her, her ponytail gleaming in the late afternoon light. The woman regarded Aida carefully. Her smiling lips curved down into something more reserved, polite. It struck Aida odd that the woman's smile didn't grow with her presence, but rather diminished.

"Mind if I sit?" Aida asked. Her knees trembled under her nightgown.

The woman looked around the park as if to survey if there were other benches available and then shifted to the far edge to create room, or distance for Aida—she couldn't tell which. Aida studied the baby, his strawberry-blonde curls that splayed from the tops of his ears in sweet ringlets. His thickly lashed blue eyes grew wide as he took Aida in.

"What a beautiful baby," Aida remarked. She kept her voice light and high even though staring at the infant gutted her. "How old is he?"

"Thank you. He's six months old." She couldn't be sure, but the woman may have pulled the baby closer to her.

"I think you live on my street. You've just moved in, right?"

The woman shifted uncomfortably. "Where do you live then?" Her voice was careful, measured.

Now that Aida was meeting this woman in person, she wasn't as friendly as her perpetual smiling face would suggest. Aida wondered what else the woman faked.

"Sunbrook Crescent." Aida smiled, her eyes reverting to the baby. Always to the baby.

The woman smiled wider this time at the connection between them. "We *are* neighbours then."

"I think you've met my husband, Marvin."

"Oh, yes, of course. Marvin!"

Aida made a clucking sound to the baby, hoping to engage him. His fists clutched his mother's shirt, and he buried his face in her chest away from Aida.

The woman's arms loosened around the baby and dropped lower onto her lap. The baby's face remained hidden. Aida's gut did somersaults. She wiggled her fingers. They were pulsing as she stared at the back of the baby's head.

"I'm Jenna." The woman grinned widely this time. Her lips revealed perfectly straight, white teeth. Aida noted her lovely skin, a creamy olive complexion free of blemishes or wrinkles. She didn't even look *tired*.

"Aida." It felt weird to say her name out loud. To claim her existence again.

"And this is Lucas." Jenna pulled the baby away from her to turn him so that Aida could see him, but he resisted her. Aida felt her heart pierce at the child's resistance. She'd give anything to interact with him. Aida marveled at his outfit—a white T-shirt under denim overalls, tiny red socks, and sneakers. A baby dressed like a little man, a miniature sailor. "I think he's tired," Jenna sounded apologetic. "He didn't have his afternoon nap today."

Aida nodded in understanding.

"Do you have kids?" Jenna's question was meant to be innocent, but it felt murderous.

"I do. A son. He's two. Tommy."

Jenna lit up. "Ooh, a playmate! Lucas would love that, wouldn't you, Lucas?" She kissed the top of his head. "I haven't met any other mothers in the neighbourhood yet. It would be so great to connect with another mom!" Aida listened for any hesitation in her voice, but Jenna sounded genuine. Her warmth surprised Aida—she didn't expect to want Jenna's attention as much as she did.

"We'd like that," Aida responded without thinking.

Lucas shifted in his mother's arms and began to fuss. Jenna bounced him on her lap again, but he rubbed his eyes and stared warily at Aida.

"Where is your son?"

"Huh?" Aida could feel the cogs in her mind slowing as Jenna's question hung in the air.

"He's with your husband, then? Napping?"

Aida's eyesight went fuzzy. Her surroundings went topsy-turvy and threatened to cave in on her. She could feel Jenna's eyes on her—studying her bare legs from under her thick coat, her unlaced running shoes. Lucas broke out into a cry. Jenna popped the plastic soother that dangled from a clip on his overalls into his mouth; he sucked vigorously for a few seconds and then spit it out. Aida was grateful for the distraction. When he let out a wail, Jenna reached down into the diaper bag in the basket on the bottom of the stroller. She pulled out a soft, cream-coloured stuffed lamb and handed it to the baby. He promptly tossed it, his frustration building.

Jenna's cheeks flushed pink. "I'm sorry," she said this time. "I'm sure you understand. He's been teething lately." She leaned in, her face suddenly so innocent and open, Aida relished the vulnerability. "Tell me, how do you ever get through it?"

Aida waved her hand. "You'll get through it too, I promise."

She couldn't believe her words. Promises were empty, impossible to keep. You could promise a lot of things, but did they ever really mean anything?

"Motherhood. It's so hard some days." Jenna's bottom lip quivered just the slightest. Enough for Aida to see fissures in the perfect façade.

Jenna soothed Lucas and rubbed his back. He calmed and even turned toward Aida. Another glimpse of his cherub face took Aida's breath away. She tried cooing at him this time, and when he finally smiled back, her whole body coursed with joy. Jenna looked pleased.

"Do you want to hold him?" Jenna asked casually. "I better get his lamb."

Aida straightened and put her arms out before Jenna could finish her sentence. Lucas stared at her warily as Jenna placed him in her arms. Aida immediately put the baby to her chest and sucked a deep breath of his hair, the sweet, delicate smell of lavender filling her nostrils. He put his hands against her and pushed away; the feel of his tiny hands on her awakened something, her mind a junked machine repaired and brought back to usefulness. She gripped him closer and stood, her legs sturdier and more certain than she'd felt in weeks.

Jenna's back was turned away from her to retrieve the lamb that Lucas had thrown. Aida's pulse quickened with opportunity. She couldn't stop herself—she swung on her heels, her feet carrying her and the baby down the path they'd come, in the direction of Sunbrook Crescent. If she were quick enough, perhaps she could find a way to spend more time with this child. Perhaps the two of them could escape somewhere far, before anyone could find them.

A baby needed someone solid, experienced—someone who knew how to handle teething and napping. Someone with so much love to give that motherhood would never feel like a burden. Aida's pace accelerated, her laces thwapping against her shins like tiny lashings. She could feel her nipples perk through her nightgown, eager to nourish and provide.

Lucas pushed against her again, eager to come back up for air from Aida's tight grip. She bounced him and made shushing noises as she strode. When she glanced down at his perfect porcelain face, he was staring up at her in stunned bewilderment.

"Lucas!" came Jenna's cry. "Aida?!" There was a slight strangle in the words. Aida could hear the uncertainty, the tinge of anguish in Jenna's voice at seeing her baby held by another woman at the edge of the park, unmoored from the safety of the park bench. Aida smiled.

When Aida got to the sidewalk that would lead them back to their crescent, she realized that she was breathing wildly, an intense wheeze that made her dizzy and disoriented. The world spun in jagged flashes of colour.

"Aida?!" This time it was a man's voice. Deep and authoritative. A parent talking to a child. Marvin. "What are you doing?!"

Aida was sure she was dreaming until she felt Lucas' little hands pressing against her breasts again. Aida blinked and Marvin came into focus, his neatly pressed charcoal suit, his tan loafers, crisp white shirt, and silky navy tie. His wavy chestnut hair flopped down into his eyes, and he pushed it back with his fingers as he caught his breath. He was a handsome man, had always been.

"This is Lucas," Aida smiled sweetly. She turned the baby to face Marvin, sure that the sight of the child, in his cute Gap outfit, a little naval captain himself, would please her husband. Marvin looked back and forth between her and the baby, his eyes bulging.

"I came in from the garage, and you weren't in the house. The front door was wide open!"

"I shut the door," Aida mumbled, sure she'd closed the door behind her. That open door betrayed her and had led Marvin to find her here. He glanced beyond his wife at the neighbour running toward them, clutching the blanket and the stuffed lamb, her face also a question mark. He put his arm around his wife, but she stiffened at his hand on her back. He did not pay attention to the baby.

"Jenna," Marvin greeted her. Aida's insides lurched. Of course, they knew one another. It was all true then, Marvin gazing out the window at her. Wishing this woman were his wife. This trusting, smiling, warm wife. This mother.

"You've met my wife then," Marvin scratched his head. Jenna snatched the baby out of Aida's hands, her eyes demanding answers. Aida felt her body shrivel again, an instant atrophy without the baby.

"We just went for a nice little walk," Aida cooed at Lucas. "Didn't we, Lucas?" Aida clapped her hands softly for the baby, but he buried his head into his mother again. "I thought I'd show him to Marvin!"

Jenna, visibly shaken, still displayed her polite smile. "Hello, Marvin." She juggled the baby in her arms. "Is this your wife?" Of course, she'd smile. Jenna's perfect teeth flashing at her husband, beckoning him for more. Marvin returned it, relieved that his wife was found, that there was no harm done. Marvin nodded.

"We should get back home, dear…" Marvin said gently. "We can make dinner together."

She couldn't remember the last time they'd prepared a meal together. The sun had dipped, the horizon now a kaleidoscope of pink and orange. Aida saw the flecks of grey in her husband's piercing gaze. She saw the violet circles that matched her own. The observation startled her.

"Nice to see you again," Marvin nodded at Jenna as he led Aida away from the park. Aida winced. Each step felt heavier the further she got from the baby; the blood in her body was thickening into sludge. Aida's gaze fixated on the baby. She waved back at him as Marvin pulled her.

Jenna's shoulders relaxed as they departed, and she grasped Lucas's slight wrist and shook it as though he were waving goodbye to the couple.

Whether it was to be courteous or a desperate bid for friendship, Jenna called out, "Aida, next time, bring Tommy!"

Marvin froze. He thought of returning to Jenna to set her straight, but the thought of saying it out loud was more than he could bear in this moment.

Marvin led them home, but he was silent the entire way. Aida chattered about Lucas' outfit, how he was teething. Marvin tuned her out, incapable of computing what she was saying.

He'd promised her things would get better, that they'd get through their loss. Now, he wasn't so sure. Marvin guided his wife through the front door of their home, their dream house, and watched as she disappeared down the hallway. He scooped up his wife's bathrobe from the living room floor, slid his shoes off, stretched his cramped toes, and rubbed his eyes.

Marvin looked around the front room and felt it cold and empty. The sun had retreated, leaving the room dim and somber. He approached the window so that he could close the blinds.

He could see his neighbour Jenna returning home, pushing the stroller down the sidewalk. Marvin watched her as she strode confidently toward her house. She looked so carefree and happy. Marvin felt the sting of jealousy grow within his gut. He couldn't see the baby, but it was probably better that way. He replayed the scene at the park in his head. For a moment, he wondered what he really saw. Surely his wife wouldn't... no, she would not. Could not.

Meanwhile, Aida opened the last door in the hallway—a room they'd avoided for months. For once, she was excited. This experience had breathed new life into her. Her breath caught in her throat at the neat letters T-O-M-M-Y tacked to the wall spelling his name, his outfits hanging neatly in the closet. She sat on the edge of his toddler bed and smoothed his comforter with her hand.

A mother needed her child to feel complete. Maybe there was hope for her and Marvin—another chance waiting for them. An opportunity when she least expected it. Aida fished for the lump in her jacket pocket. She pulled out the stuffed lamb, the one Lucas had thrown, now streaked with dirt. Jenna hadn't noticed that she'd dropped it when she grabbed Lucas back from her. Aida tucked the lamb into the covers, pulling the blankets under the toy's chin. She patted the covers with satisfaction and rose to join her husband. They were going to make dinner tonight.

As Aida stepped through the hallway, she took in the handsomeness of her living room: the Eames chair, the tufted couch, the Stonington Gray paint. She decided it looked chic after all. That is, until she saw Marvin standing at the blinds, gazing at his neighbour, just as she had predicted.

Boschuk Family
Medicine

Dr. Gordon Boschuk smoothed his grey dress shirt and made sure it was still tucked into his pants before opening the door to the next examination room. His snow-white hair was combed neatly into soft waves. His spotted skin was a rich golden hue from early mornings on the golf course. Kind, sky-blue eyes peered out from his bifocals.

"Hello Irma, what brings you in today?" Gordon had a hunch it was more apt to be loneliness after losing her husband Frank this past year than a measurable change in health.

"You know how it goes," Irma shook her head. "I'm getting older, and nothing works the same anymore."

Gordon nodded. He could agree on that. Aging was a bitch. First, it had been his eyes, then his knees. He'd had to give up running almost two decades ago. Otherwise, for seventy-four, he'd weathered the years pretty well. Better than most.

Irma shuffled her way to the examining table. At 4'11 and 95 pounds, she was a wisp of a thing. Her short silver hair was curled in perfect mounds around her head. She'd put on cherry lipstick.

"I've been having some trouble with my one leg." Irma stretched her right leg in front of her. It trembled from the effort of keeping it raised.

"What kind of trouble?"

"I'm noticing that I'm stumbling a lot. That it doesn't seem to do what I want it to do."

Gordon noted the tremble on his clipboard.

"Let's check your vitals, first." He listened to her with his stethoscope. The flash of the diamonds in Irma's wedding ring caught his eye as he listened. Frank's death had taken them all by surprise—he'd had a massive heart attack in the middle of the night.

Irma's lungs were clear. Her heart was unremarkable.

He checked her pedal pulse to confirm circulation to the foot. Next, he'd check her motor response and mobility. At eighty-two, deficiencies in mobility were commonplace.

"Can you wiggle your foot for me? Side to side?"

Irma's foot was visible through her taupe stockings. Gordon could follow the blue veins down her leg to the curve of her bunions and to her claw-like toes. They were painted the colour of her lipstick—the very tips showed tinges of yellow nails. He placed his hand against the base of her foot. Irma blushed at his touch.

"Can you push down like a gas pedal for me? Now pull back away from my hand." He had her repeat the action several times, out, in, out, in. Gordon reached for a tongue depressor, snapped it in half, and poked her feet and toes.

"Can you feel it here?" Irma nodded each time he pressed the jagged end gently against her skin. "Well, your sensation and nerve stimuli seem good. I wonder if it isn't the Warfarin we put you on last visit. Muscle weakness is a side effect of the medication. Any other changes?" The more information a doctor had the better. Every piece could aid in putting together the puzzle. "Any dizziness? Hair loss? Rashes?"

"No," Irma said. "Just my leg." She patted it.

"Well, let's lower your dose for now and see how things go. Maybe see you in a month?"

Irma nodded, but she made no move to leave. Gordon set down his clipboard.

"How are you getting on?" Gordon asked. "Since Frank, I mean…"

Irma's eyes filled with tears. She launched into what her days were like without him. Gordon settled into his chair.

❖ ❖ ❖

"Dad, everything okay in here?" A younger version of Gordon peeked his head around the door. Mark was the other half of the father-son duo who made up the medical practice of Boschuk Family Medicine.

"Mark! I was just telling Irma here about Ariel." Ariel was Mark's three-year-old daughter, Gordon's only grandchild.

"Hello, Mrs. Porter. Nice to see you again." Mark smiled at Irma, but it didn't reach his blue eyes. Mark motioned for his dad to come closer. "There is a roomful of patients waiting. You're running about an hour behind."

"Sounds like Janine overbooked."

Mark scratched his head. Their medical office assistant, Janine, had been with them for years. She was the real backbone of the place, the way she kept everything together. Mark highly doubted that Janine had made a mistake.

"Want me to take any of them for you?" Mark offered. He knew his dad would say no. Sometimes he still thought of Mark as a student doctor even though he'd been practicing a decade now. Gordon's eyebrows rose.

"I can see them all myself, thank you." His words were clipped.

Mark checked his watch and waved to Mrs. Porter. He strode out to the waiting room and nodded to the remaining patients. Janine had left long before—she was off at four p.m. every day and it was after five now. Mark spotted the patient charts stacked neatly in the tray. Just seeing the manila files sent his blood pumping. The entire province had moved to an electronic system years ago, but his dad was adamant that they keep things the way they'd always been done. He claimed he was too old to learn new tricks, that technology was not reliable the way paper was.

Mark was taking more of the patients these days. This was intentional. His dad had been the town's beloved doctor for near fifty years, but he had no intentions of slowing down. At his age, Mark thought it was time. He wanted his dad to step aside and leave the practice in his more-than-capable hands.

Mark phoned home to let his wife Lily know that he'd be late.

"Again?"

"He's just finishing up with the last couple patients." Mark couldn't tell her there were still five more waiting. He didn't like to leave his dad at the clinic by himself. He set his stethoscope on his desk and sat in his leather office chair. He couldn't keep coming home late, seeing after his dad. He needed a way to convince his dad to retire.

Mark grabbed the stack of paperwork waiting for him on his desk and flipped through it—most of it was lab and radiology results that Janine had printed off for him. He looked for any abnormalities and decided he'd call the patients back himself. He'd be waiting at the clinic anyhow, and he knew that the patients always appreciated the extra care of hearing his voice rather than Janine's.

His phone rang before he could finish dialing the first number.

"Dr. Mark Boschuk, Boschuk Family Medicine."

"Hello, this is Lane Maxwell, from Endocrinology." Dr. Maxwell was the endocrinologist in Saskatoon that they referred patients to most.

"Oh, right, Lane. How are you? What can I do for you?"

"I'm wondering if Gordon is available?"

"He's with patients right now. Anything I can help you with?"

"I … well, you see…" Lane cleared his throat. "I'm confused about a patient referral I received from him. I think there must be some paperwork missing?"

"Who's that?" Mark asked. In their town of approximately 1200, he'd know who the patient was.

"Annie Lewis?"

Mark knew Annie well. They'd practically grown up together; her family had lived across from his since they were toddlers.

"I'm familiar with Annie," Mark said.

"Well, you see, the thing is—her labs show nothing too concerning. Just that her iron stores are low. I wouldn't recommend anything else here but taking an iron supplement. I'm not sure why she was referred to me."

Mark jotted down notes and tapped his pencil on his desk.

"I'll see if there's anything missing or if something else didn't make it over there."

"Thanks, I'd appreciate that."

The two bid each other goodbye. Mark pulled Annie Lewis' file, but the most current notes were the referral and the lab work Lane had mentioned. He could not see anything else, and iron at these levels did not merit a referral to a specialist. Mark made a note to ask his dad about it. He hoped there was more to the story, but he wasn't sure anymore. There'd been more and more of these little slips—small decisions that didn't quite add up. His phone buzzed, signalling a text.

It was from Lily. *If you're not here in fifteen minutes, I'll put your dinner in the fridge.*

Mark rubbed his eyes before typing back.

I'll be there right away.

He shifted in his seat, felt a knot in his upper back: a small stab when he moved. It was just enough to let him know a bigger pain could be brewing if he didn't get it worked out.

❖ ❖ ❖

It was 6:30 p.m. when Gordon finished with his last patient of the day. No one had been upset about waiting. In fact, Gordon got the sense that his patients loved chatting with him about their families. That was one of the things that had led him back to his hometown. He'd occupied the tidy, compact orange brick building on the corner of Main and 2nd Street since 1965 as a newly minted graduate of the University of Saskatchewan. He'd purchased the building outright with an inheritance from his grandmother.

Returning to Outlook had always been his plan. He'd hated how his fellow graduates always set out for the big cities when smaller communities needed them. He took no joy from the fast pace of the city and how rushed he'd felt there; there were always more patients than any clinic could reasonably handle. Not only was there a constant stream of patients to see, but the time allotted to each of them was not nearly enough. He preferred more time to get to know his patients—ask them about their lives and hear the backstory about what brought them to him. Practicing in the city could not give him that.

And now Mark was breathing down his neck every day, wanting to change everything. He couldn't be happy with the practice that had worked just fine for the past five decades. Instead, Mark wanted to automate things, streamline the office, *modernize* as he called it. Gordon didn't see the point. It would mean that they would see more patients in a shorter frame of time, thereby erasing what set him apart from the clinics in the city; all in the name of *efficiency*—another word Mark used that Gordon hated.

"Can we go now?" Mark rubbed his temples from the front door, his keys dangling from the deadbolt, poised for action.

"No one is holding you here, Mark." Gordon said. He tried to remember the last time he'd gone home on his own. Mark seemed to lock up after him every day. Did his son think he couldn't close up? Gordon gave his son a once over. "Tuck in your shirt, will you? Try to look professional."

Mark looked down at his cobalt slim-fit button down. It was a casual but handsome shirt in a fun print. It wasn't meant to be tucked in. Mark turned his key in the lock to the clinic and watched his dad struggle into his blue late model Camry. He slid into the driver's seat of his black BMW. He wondered if his dad should still be driving, but any mention of giving up his license was another bone of contention between them.

Mark watched his dad turn off Main Street toward his home, while he continued to the edge of town to the custom home he'd built with his wife. As he approached the sleek, charcoal-sided two-story, he pictured his chilled meal on the top shelf of the fridge. He pressed the garage door opener and parked the car for the night. When he came through the garage and into the house, Ariel came running.

"Daddy!" She jumped into his outstretched arms. Strands of her honey-coloured hair sprung from the braids that had been tightly plaited that morning. Mark scooped her up and breathed in the smell of peaches. Lily gave him a half-hearted smile and sat at their dining room table; she had her arms crossed in front of her. Her tawny blunt-cut bob covered her jawline, but Mark knew she was clenching her teeth. The table was set, the meal waiting still.

"Sorry I'm late, Lil." Mark approached her and bent to kiss her forehead.

"I hope it's not cold," Lily replied. Her lips pursed. "Maybe I should stop making dinner at all. He only finished with those patients now?" Lily asked. Mark nodded and scooped chicken and quinoa salad onto his plate.

"When are you going to talk to him?"

"I have, Lil. You know that."

"No, I mean, *really* talk to him. He can't practice anymore, Mark. You know it, I know it."

"I got a call today. From an endocrinologist in Saskatoon. Says Dad referred someone to him for low iron. Wondered if there'd been paperwork missing or something."

"But let me guess. There wasn't."

"Not that I could see."

"This is what I'm talking about, Mark. Something's going to happen. And then what?"

"Nothing's going to happen, Lily. I've got this. I'll take over as much as I can until we can convince him to retire."

Lily cut her chicken, and the knife made a loud screech against her plate.

"At least do it before 5 p.m. then," she sighed. "That's the whole reason we agreed to settle here instead of the city, Mark. A quieter life, a better schedule. It feels like that was short-lived."

This was also dangerous territory, this allegiance he held to both his wife and his father; he felt like he couldn't satisfy either one of them or make them understand what he was juggling. Lily was right—they'd settled in Outlook for the sole purpose of a quieter life. One where Lily could work on her art and they could raise Ariel—their beloved child who'd been born after four failed IVF attempts. He, himself, had a great childhood in the town, and it had been important to him and Lily to have any potential children get to know their grandfather. Lily's parents lived way out in Texas and Mark's mother had passed several years earlier. Joining the practice with his dad seemed so natural at the time. Ten years in, however, it felt like a different story.

A week later, Irma Porter returned to the clinic. Her leg was still bothering her. Lowering the dose of the blood thinner did nothing to change the instability she was experiencing. Gordon repeated the same tests he'd done the week before.

"Well, I think I should refer you to the city for an ultrasound. See if there could be a blood clot forming." Gordon said, his hand tucked under his chin. He studied Irma's leg. There was no tenderness to the touch, no redness or swelling. He was sure she was coming in just to visit. He knew what losing your spouse was like—how lonely and disorienting those first years were. He'd been with Vera since he was eighteen years old. He'd spent more of his life with her than without her. She'd been everything to him. Losing her to breast cancer like they had was crushing for all of them. Gordon wasn't sure he'd ever be able to move on. Though she'd died ten years earlier, he felt the weight of grief robbing him of his breath still, and in the most unpredictable moments. It was easier to keep busy than to sit by himself in the terrifying silence of their home. He imagined that Irma was experiencing the same without Frank.

Gordon wrote out a requisition for her. She accepted it and wiggled herself off the examination table. He watched, surprised, as Irma shuffled to the hallway. There would be no extra talk between them today. He might leave on time. The thought unnerved him. Mark had his family to go home to; Gordon had an empty house full of reminders of Vera. There, at home, Gordon was nothing but a grieving husband, a man who could barely keep himself clothed and fed properly in the absence of his wife.

Mark left as soon as he knew the patients were all taken care of. Gordon didn't like Mark's desire to leave the clinic as soon as he could. He didn't think his son had the same dedication to the field and the practice that he had. Mark had had it easy; he'd finished medical school with a golden opportunity: to practice alongside his father in an ideal setting in a community perfect for raising children.

Things hadn't worked out as Gordon had hoped though. Mark and Lily had only ever had one child in all these years, and Vera had never been alive to see her. He'd wanted scores of grandchildren running around. He hoped that Boschuk Family Medicine could stand the test of time—his original clinic still helping people for generations to come. He loved it when Ariel visited the clinic. He let her play with the instruments; she loved to look inside her grandpa's ears and listen to his irregular heartbeat. He called her his intern—baby Dr. Boschuk, and Ariel didn't even mind him referring to her as a baby.

Mark hadn't brought Ariel by in weeks. He and Mark weren't getting along as well as they used to. He thought Mark maybe needed a break. A vacation. Time to let go of some of the stress he was carrying, though Gordon could not see what his son could be stressed about.

"Dr. Boschuk, I've got Pharmacy on line two for you," Janine said from the end of the hallway. She greeted Mrs. Porter as she passed her in the hallway.

Gordon nodded. "I'll take it in my office." He grabbed the receiver on his desk.

"Dr. Gordon Boschuk here," he said. His voice was deep, gruff. It carried an authority that had served him well over the years.

"Gordon, hello," It was Darla from the pharmacy down the street.

"What can I do for you today?"

"I have a prescription you wrote here for Brody Winters. It says here you want him to take 20 milligrams of Dilaudid twice a day. I think there must've been a mistake. Seems a little high, no?"

"That was supposed to be a two. I must've forgotten the decimal," Gordon chuckled. "My mistake."

Darla laughed as well. "I figured that couldn't be right. I'll go ahead and fill this then. Sorry to bother you."

"Not a problem, Darla. By the way, how are your kids doing?"

Darla was more than happy to chat with him. Gordon sank back into his leather office chair and twirled the phone cord in his hands.

Lily called Mark to tell him that Ariel wasn't feeling well. They'd run out of Tylenol. Mark would stop at the pharmacy on the way home.

The bells jingled above the door when he pulled it open. The plump and bubbly woman with permed and frosted hair waved at him from the back of the little store.

"Hi, Darla. Lily called. Ariel's got a fever, I guess," Mark said. A minute later, he placed a bottle of Tylenol and a litre of apple juice on the counter.

"Aw, poor thing," Darla clucked. "I just finished talking to your dad actually."

"Oh, yeah?"

"Maybe I shouldn't say anything, but I thought it was kind of weird."

"What's that?" Mark said. He was looking at the brand-new point-of-sale system the pharmacy had installed. Even Darla's family, the original owners of the pharmacy, believed in updating to current standards. Why couldn't his dad do the same?

"Well, see, your dad wrote a prescription, but I was sure it was a mistake."

Darla tipped her head toward him and brought her voice down low.

"It was for Dilaudid." Darla straightened and looked around the store even though they were the only ones inside.

"Okay," Mark said slowly. Lots of patients were on Dilaudid.

"The thing is, it said 20 milligrams." That wasn't unheard of; it all depended on the patient and the medical issue. He still didn't get the problem.

"It was for Brody Winters and his sprain."

This time, Mark nodded. Brody was the high school quarterback. News of his injury spread fast because it meant he'd be sitting on the sidelines this season.

"It actually was a break, not a sprain. But you're right, that had to be a mistake. That must've been a two," Mark said quickly.

"Yes, that's what he said, that he forgot to add a decimal between the two and the zero, but I'll show you … I've got it right here…"

Darla retrieved the prescription and smoothed it out for Mark to see. There, in his dad's careful script was the word 'twenty', spelled out in letters instead of numbers. He had not forgotten a decimal. Mark blinked. His face grew hot. Giving that kind of dose to a young opiate-naïve patient could be disastrous, fatal even.

"It's not the first time I've had to clarify," Darla whispered.

Mark's face flamed. He moved his lips to respond, but his tongue felt like sandpaper in his mouth.

"We all love him, Mark." Darla put her hand on his and studied him. Her eyes softened. Mark could feel his bottom lip quiver. "We also know how stubborn that man can be." Mark nodded, numb. He snatched the juice and the Tylenol and turned back toward the entrance. He worried that if he stayed a minute longer, he'd burst into tears.

Later that night, Mark decided it was time to have the talk again. Initially, he thought of doing it over the phone, but his dad might hang up on him. His dad needed to be shown how serious this was—how much this affected the community he loved—and so it needed to happen face to face.

The windows of his father's house were dim; there were no signs of light from within. Mark checked the clock on the dashboard. It was only 7:15 p.m. It was unlikely that his dad was asleep already. The red brick character home he'd grown up in was still charming. His dad had gone to great lengths to find the right people to care for the yard and his mother's rosebushes and apple trees after she passed.

When Mark entered the house, there was no sign of his dad. He called out to him. There was no answer. He moved from room to room, but they were all empty. Mark's heart started to pound. His dad was relatively healthy and fit, but he had atrial fibrillation. His heart problems could get worse. He half expected to find his dad on the floor somewhere. He picked up his pace and checked the basement and the backyard. He walked out to the detached garage at the end of the long driveway and peered through the window. It was empty.

Mark hopped back into his car and drove up and down some of the streets where his dad's friends lived, hoping to spot his navy-blue Camry. He didn't know why he felt so unsettled. His dad was an independent man. He didn't need a babysitter, he just needed to retire from practicing medicine. When Mark reached Main and 2nd Street, he shook his head. His dad's Camry was parked beside the burnt wood clinic sign: *Boschuk Family Medicine*.

Mark parked behind his dad's car and entered the building. The lights were on inside as if they were open for business. The door was unlocked. Mark called for his dad once he stood in the doorway. He didn't want to startle the poor man; they didn't have bells to signal someone's arrival like the pharmacy.

He heard nothing. Mark looked around the empty office and felt a swell of pride. His dad had built an amazing business for the two of them—a practice that had benefitted the community in many ways. He'd never lost his dad's vision for the place; he just wanted to make some much-needed changes. Mark heard a sniffle from his dad's office.

"Dad?" Mark called out softly. He peered into his dad's office and found him sitting on the floor, his back against the wall.

"Dad! What's wrong?" Mark ran to him. Gordon's legs were outstretched and his shiny black oxford shoes had been kicked off. Even his shirt was untucked. Gordon waved him off.

"I'm fine," he said. But his eyes were rimmed with red. His cheeks were blotchy. Mark realized that his dad had been crying.

"Are you hurt? In pain?" Mark's heart quickened. "Is it your heart?"

He wasn't used to seeing his dad cry.

"No, Son. I'm fine." But he wasn't.

"What are you doing here?" Mark knelt beside him and looked around the room. He wondered if his dad was drunk. He looked for a bottle of alcohol but saw none. Everything was in its place. Gordon's desk was clear. His stethoscope was curled like a snake on the corner of it.

Gordon grabbed his son's collar and pulled him close, knocking Mark off his stance. Mark braced himself using the wall and sat closer to his dad. He winced when his back met the wall. The knot grew warm and started to pulsate.

"I'm nothing if I'm not a doctor here," Gordon's voice was low, tortured.

"Dad… come on… don't say that," Mark broke in. "You're an amazing man. You've got us, Ariel, your friends. The whole community loves you."

Gordon shook his head. "It's not enough," he said. The words pierced Mark. They felt like knives in his chest. "This," he threw his hands up and gestured to the walls around him. "It's what I was born to do," he managed. His voice cracked.

"And it's what you *have* done. Wonderfully. There's no shame in hanging up the coat."

Gordon put his head in his hands and wept. His shoulders curled. Mark pulled him into a hug. He ignored the throbbing pain in his own back, wrapped his arms around the old man, felt him shudder and shake. Gordon's breath blew in ragged gasps between his sobs. His dad felt distinctly small and vulnerable in his arms, as though Mark had become the steady force, the protector.

"I think I killed Frank Porter." Gordon said it so quietly, Mark might have imagined it.

"He died of a heart attack, Dad."

"But I didn't send him to Saskatoon. Maybe a stent would have helped."

"How so?" Mark's skin prickled. He wasn't sure he could handle an admission like this, but Gordon didn't answer. He continued to sob. Mark rubbed his back and let his dad cry. They sat together until Gordon cried himself to sleep.

Mark lowered his dad back toward the floor and reached for the desk to steady himself and get back on his feet. He took a flannel coverlet from the supply cupboard and placed it over his dad. Seeing him curled in a fetal position with his hair out of place, his shirt untucked, and in his stocking feet, stunned him. He looked more like a young child than his formidable dad.

Mark's mind spun. He needed to see Frank Porter's chart. Mark walked to the filing cabinet and searched under the letter "P". He knew that even though he'd passed, his file would still be in the cabinet. He spotted Frank's chart and sat in Janine's office chair. He combed through Frank's medical history quickly, preferring to fixate on the final pages. He saw Frank's last ECG and the last labs taken before his death. He'd presented with chest pain according to his dad's familiar scrawl. Mark reviewed the labs: saw the elevated troponin in Frank's bloodwork, the ST segment elevation on his ECG, signaling that one or more vessels were occluded—all the evidence needed to indicate a heart attack. Mark felt the colour drain from his face. His dad was right. Not sending Frank Porter to Saskatoon for an emergency stent was a mistake. It likely cost him his life.

Mark pictured his dad, curled into a ball on the floor in his office after hours. He wondered how many nights he might have lain there, while Mark was home with his family. He knew his dad had never really rebounded after the loss of Mark's mom, Vera. He thought of other losses in his dad's life. Losses that would only compound with time. Mark took the final ECG and lab work out of the file. He placed the file back under the "P" section of the filing cabinet. He took the incriminating information and fed it into the top slot of the shredder and listened as the machine sucked it down. He returned to his dad, gently shook him awake and helped him to his feet.

"Let's get you dressed." Mark tucked in his dad's shirt and smoothed it. He ran his fingers through his dad's soft white hair, pulled his socks up, and placed his feet into his shoes. Mark tied the delicate laces and reached for his dad's hand.

"We've got to get you home, Dr. Boschuk. You've got a big day tomorrow. I looked in the book. I see your slots are full."

You Are Not Who You Used to Be

Aurora Lewis set down her Louis Vuitton suitcase—a luxury item in a spartan room. This wasn't a vacation, but an opportunity to work undisturbed and undistracted. She'd been stuck for weeks and with the looming deadline from her publisher, progress needed to happen now. This week at the Wellspring Creative Retreat Centre promised a break from her uninspired existence. Her time would be her own to use as she pleased. She hoped it would be fruitful.

Aurora had found quick success in publishing her first two romance novels. For her third, she was writing under deadline. It was the first time she'd ever written this way, and she found it stifling and pressure-inducing. Over the past several weeks, she'd written dozens of openings that she was initially hopeful about, but when she returned to them the next day, she felt as deflated as the writing and promptly deleted them. There were no ideas about what she'd write about; no sizzling story lines paving the way.

Aurora unpacked her toiletries and lined them along the cool porcelain counter in the bathroom. Her fingers worked to set the labels on the bottles just the right way. She hung her coat in the tiny closet and lined up her shoes directly beneath her coat. She pulled out her clunky laptop and set it on the old wooden desk. She flicked on the small desk lamp provided by the retreat centre and added the pretty, but outrageously priced pencil case she'd ordered online. It was shell pink and had red hearts all over it. It looked like something an eight-year-old would love, but she'd seen it and as a romance writer, she felt she had to have it. When it arrived in the mail, it was made of heavy plastic when she'd expected leather for that price. But it was still pretty, even if she'd been ripped off. Now it housed her favourite supplies. She twisted open the blinds and let the sun flood the space. This open spell of alone time before her meant that for the first time in months, there was possibility in the room. Characters unmet, story lines to be woven, futures to be determined.

Mid-afternoon, Aurora opened her door to find herself face to face with a man coming out of the room directly across from hers. Their eyes locked immediately, steadfast and binding. This was not just a polite appraisal of one another, but an electric current burning so intensely, Aurora felt as though she might combust. Her breath was taken from her. His sparkling cobalt eyes bored into hers. She wondered if he was just as shocked by this sudden collision of energies.

"Hi, I'm Aurora," she stammered. She knew her face was flushed with colour; she could feel her cheeks flooding with warmth. She wished she'd smoothed her hair and checked herself in the mirror before exiting her room.

"Michael," he said. He held his hand out to shake hers. The ends of her fingers tingled when they touched. She returned the handshake, the blood in her hands and arms pumped vigorously. She wanted to take him in, drink in all his features, but she ducked her head and continued down the hallway instead. His presence had made her heart quicken and she lost her breath—a full fight or flight sensation coursed through her.

Later, when the retreatants met for dinner, she chose the spot furthest from him, unaware of anyone else in the room. She hoped she'd be able to steal glances at him—study the creature that had unnerved her in this way. He was deep in conversation with others around the table and Aurora was grateful to peer at him unnoticed. He wore a plain long-sleeved black Henley top and simple khaki pants, which felt too plain and serious for an artist. Was he a writer too?

She looked for a wedding ring on his hand but found none. He brushed a chestnut brown curl behind his ears before starting into his dessert. His piercing eyes crinkled when he laughed. She couldn't place his age. There were tinges of silver at his temples. Otherwise, his face had a youthfulness to it. He hadn't experienced the ravages of aging like she had. Just as she spooned the last of her bread pudding into her mouth, their eyes caught once again, and that same heat lit her from within. She blushed, looked away, and rose to clear her spot at the table as quickly as she could.

She'd never experienced an instant attraction like this, and certainly not with her husband, David. The initial attraction between them felt lukewarm at best when compared to the tingling sensations she felt upon meeting Michael. She'd found David good looking, sure, but she'd never experienced this animal-like hormonal surge even once in the years they'd been together.

Back in her room, Aurora turned on her computer, hoping for something to make sense within her and release a torrent of words. Instead, she was hyper aware of the footsteps that shuffled outside the door. It was him, returning to his room. She heard the click of his door closing behind him and tried to picture what he was doing. She pictured him with his elbow propped on the desk, his fingers nestled in his curls. His thick lashes pointed to the sky, a slight curl at the edge of the fringe. Was Michael imagining her?

Instead of writing, Aurora set to cleaning herself up. She pulled out the makeup bag she almost hadn't brought with her—after all, she was supposed to be holed up in this little room writing—but was now grateful for the last-minute addition to her suitcase. She applied a pale pink blush to her fair skin and coated her eyelashes with black mascara. She studied her face in the mirror. Since she'd turned forty, crow's feet had taken residence beside her eyes and frown lines were embedded in her forehead. She pulled her skin back in both places and wished for the smooth complexion of her youth.

Her once-sculpted jawline sagged and hung like dog jowls. The loose and wrinkled skin travelled down her neck until it hit her collarbone. Aurora rubbed her cheeks, admonishing herself. "Why did I think he'd possibly find me attractive?" Aurora whispered to the mirror. "You, Aurora, are not who you used to be." She noted her arms hugging herself in the reflection. Shivers reverberated down her spine. She felt the urge to cry.

Her cell phone pinged with a text message. She took a deep breath. She knew without looking that it was David. She stared at her phone as it lit up multiple times from its perch on the desk. Aurora put away her cosmetics and pulled her slippers and a cardigan from her suitcase. She wanted the feeling of soft things wrapped around her body to comfort her from the sting of negative self-talk. She plucked her phone.

Where do we keep the iron? David texted.

How do I wash Kyla's leotard for dance?

Did you pay the plumbing bill?

Aurora could feel her teeth grind. These texts were not helping her settle in to write.

Top shelf of the linen closet.

I washed the pink one. It's folded on the top of her laundry basket.

Yes, I paid it on Thursday. Aurora pressed the letters with more force than she intended. She could feel her eyebrows rising to further engrave those frown lines.

She wants to wear the purple one. David wrote back. Of course, she did. The one Aurora hadn't set out. She placed her head in her hands; her elbows propped on the desk. She decided that if she were going to get anything done this week, she'd need to fully immerse herself. She set her phone to silent and tossed it into her purse.

A thin, flowery bedspread, likely a hotel chain castoff, covered the twin bed. Aurora hadn't slept in a bed so small since she was nine. She settled herself under the covers and napped. When she woke, she gazed out at the expansive clear-blue sky from the large window, doodled absently on loose leaf with coloured markers, and counted the soap beads in the glass canister on the sill of the porcelain sink. She wanted to believe that these actions were all priming the pump of her creative well, but there was nothing bubbling and percolating inside of her.

❖ ❖ ❖

The next morning, she sat across from Michael, and to her surprise, caught him looking at her several times during the group meal. Each time, she lost her breath and her belly fluttered. The idea that he was examining her thrilled her. His gaze raised the hair on her arms. Being able to see him at close range, she noticed an umber spot, likely a birthmark, on the curve of his left cheekbone. Aurora fixated on it, imagined brushing her lips across it before kissing him. She felt like a lovesick teenager. She heard enough of the conversation to learn that he was a poet. She'd never been with another person in the creative arts such as herself. Every time she saw him, she imagined being with him to be intensely sensual—the physical meeting of creative minds.

When Aurora returned to her room, she found herself finally writing. She opened a fresh document on her laptop and started weaving a similar tale—of a woman who'd been feeling lost who meets a man at a retreat centre and feels an instant attraction to him. And for the first time in weeks, she wrote. She wrote until she felt breathless herself, until there were no words left.

That evening, after several solid hours of writing, both she and Michael opened their doors at the same time. Aurora hoped he'd planned it that way. They fell into step with one another toward the dining room.

"What are you working on?" she asked.

"A poetry manuscript," he answered. His voice was deep, gravelly. Sexy. "How about you?" As he said it, he turned his head toward her. She caught his eyes roaming over her body. Again, she studied the spot on his cheek and felt herself grow warm. His eyes felt like they burned holes through her; that he could see everything there was to her. Especially the intricacies that David could not.

"I'm under deadline for my next novel. It hasn't been going that well so far…" Aurora thought it better to tell the truth. "I was hoping some time away from my family would help."

"Married? Kids?"

She nodded.

"Two. Kyla and Jada, ages thirteen and eleven. You?"

She noticed she hadn't mentioned David.

Michael's eyes shifted to the ground. "Yes. Two. Four-year-old twins."

Aurora smiled. "Twins! Wow—that's a whole other level of busy. Great age though." She meant it. Four had felt like such a magical age with her children. There'd been few tantrums at that age and a growing inquisitiveness within them that made her feel like she was re-learning the world alongside them through their eyes.

"Having any luck with your manuscript?" Aurora asked.

"It's slow going so far," Michael admitted. They reached the dining room and found themselves reaching for the same plate.

Their hands touched and that same electric current coursed through Aurora. She gasped, then hoped it hadn't been audible. Michael smiled at her, his grin unveiling perfect white teeth. She apologized quickly and he laughed. "Nothing to worry about. Please, take this one." He held it out to her.

He chose his items from the buffet line quickly, and she watched him take a seat as she made her way down the line. She decided to sit directly across from him again, hoping to continue their conversation. He looked pleased when she sat down.

"Tell me more about you, Aurora."

She shifted uncomfortably in her seat. Even the way he said her name made her knees wobble. When he looked at her, she felt like he'd undressed her with his eyes. She couldn't remember the last time she felt so desirable. She bit her lip, wondering if she was misreading him. She knew what she saw in the mirror. How could he see something else? But she felt the weight of his eyes and his smile when she spoke. She watched his jaw as he chewed his food; his lips glistened from the salad oil. She pictured herself tasting the savoury dressing by kissing the plump of his bottom lip and felt a stirring she'd been missing for months.

"Well, this is my third novel. I'd hoped to branch out into something more daring, but my editor's not too keen on change."

"Like what?" Michael's eyes shone. "I'd love to hear more. I think a creative mind should never be stifled. The world could use a good shake up, don't you think?" The way he worded it made Aurora laugh.

"I don't think I'm looking to make that big a shake up," she said. "I think I'd just like to take more risks creatively. My editor nixed all my ideas but one. And now I can't seem to follow through."

"That's tough. Ever think of shopping your work elsewhere?"

"Not really. At least not yet. So far, this place has been helping pay the bills, you know?"

Aurora couldn't tell him that every piece she'd ever sent to a literary magazine had been rejected, let alone the dozens of manuscripts she kept tucked in her office. At this point, she felt lucky she'd ever nabbed a publishing contract at all, no matter the genre. They settled into easy conversation as they walked with one another back to their rooms.

In the dim and quiet hallway, Aurora had visions of him pressing her into the winter-white cinder block wall, his hand at the small of her back, the other brushing strands of her golden hair from her eyes before kissing her. She could imagine the warm dance of his tongue in her mouth, and it made her feel weak. Instead, he waved and twisted open the handle to his door. Aurora felt her face fall.

He's not going to just pin you down and ravage you here, Aurora. Get a grip.

Just as she was about to close her door, he called for her. Her heart quickened at the sound of her name.

"Yeah?" She peeked out the side of the door.

"Don't sell yourself short," he smiled and winked. "You've got more in you than you think."

She stuttered, unable to form a coherent reply before finally waving at him in thanks. She shut the door and sank to the floor, her back against the wooden door.

When her legs felt steadier, she set herself in front of her computer and wrote. Again, the words came easily and quickly. A confidence built in her gut. Love triangles and forbidden love were tropes that readers loved. The tension between characters who had feelings for one another but couldn't act on them had fueled some of the best love stories of all time. She could feel her editor smiling in approval with every word she wrote.

She decided to turn on her cell phone. She wouldn't be able to live with herself if she'd missed an emergency, though she knew David could call the retreat centre directly if he really needed her. As soon as she powered up her phone, a barrage of notifications came through immediately. She scrolled through the mountain of texts. Most were questions from David, funny memes from the kids, a heartfelt goodnight message from Jada that brought tears to her eyes.

She typed in a couple of replies. David responded instantly.

You don't even have time to respond to me? Nice, Aurora.

He was angry. Instead of feeling guilt, Aurora felt her own eyes flash. It may have been rude to shut off her phone, but she couldn't do what she came here to do if she were being pulled back to the running of their home dozens of times a day. David had no idea what was happening right now. This was when she needed him at his best. She needed to see his love and devotion in plain view, with an extra emphasis on how hard it was to function in her absence. But not for how to wash leotards. She wanted to know he missed her and couldn't live without her—that he *needed* her as his life partner and that he couldn't wait for her to get back to them. Because he *desired* her.

Here she was, four hours away from home, daydreaming about being with another man. One who saw her in a whole new light. She wasn't just "Mom" or wife to an insurance broker. David had always been a steady provider, which was something she loved about him, but everything he did was based on predictability and routine. David's life mission was always to bet on the side of safety and to avoid risk at all costs. She couldn't remember the last time she'd had tantalizing conversation with her husband that didn't centre on the children or work. In her current life, there was no room for wild.

At the retreat centre, Aurora wasn't the minivan driving soccer chauffeur, the treasurer of parent council, homeroom mom for 7B at Lakeview School. Here, there was an air of mystery to her—

another side to her that was sophisticated, unbridled, and free from labels and responsibilities. She was a creative professional on a mission. Mysterious and desirable. And another man was seeing her—really seeing her in the way she longed to be seen.

No time for this, David. Talk to you later. She typed back. She didn't know how he'd take that. That was the thing about texting. Things could be misconstrued or interpreted in many ways without the inflections of voice and accompanying body language. And she wasn't even sure how she meant it, but she felt fairly sure he wasn't going to be happy with her reply.

The following morning, all the retreatants but Michael gathered in the dining room for breakfast. Aurora's shoulders slumped when she realized that he wouldn't be joining them. She hadn't bothered to talk to anyone else but him since she arrived. She wasn't even that hungry. She rescued a muffin from her plate and abandoned the rest of her breakfast. Maybe he'd slept in late, and she'd catch him on the walk back to her room.

She heard the padding of his slippers before she saw him turn down the corridor. Something about seeing him in his lounge clothes and slippers clenched at her heart. It felt intimate in this public setting, and he lit up when he saw her.

"Back at it, already?" He flashed another smile.

"Time's ticking," she laughed. "I feel like Cinderella living the dream before the stroke of midnight."

"I'm sorry I missed breakfast with you then," Michael said. His words made her somersault inside.

"Hope there's still food in there, sleepyhead," she teased.

"And miss out on those gelatinous eggs? Looks like you had the right idea." He pointed at the muffin in her hand. "See you later then?"

Aurora's words lodged in her throat. She hoped so.

Aurora had another fruitful writing day. She wrote until her fingers were sore from typing and her body ached in all the best places. She wondered if the sexual tension she felt between her and Michael was the true fuel for her writing. Her muse. If so, how could she return to her regular life?

That night, after the evening meal, there was a large group of newly arrived artists at the centre, filling the hallways. Michael guided Aurora back to their rooms. He even placed his hand on the small of her back. His fingers sent pulses through her whole body. As they arrived at their rooms, she revisited the fantasy of him pressing her against the wall. When he removed his hand from her back, she found herself reaching for his arm as though to keep close to him somehow. Her fingers grazed the hairs on his forearm. His eyes grew wider for an instant and then she watched them narrow and darken with desire. Her heart hammered in her chest. She wanted to push him into his room and lower herself onto his bed, onto him. She imagined her hair falling around his face, tickling his cheeks and the groan of pleasure he'd emit just before they gave in to one another.

"Good luck, then…" she said, awkward. She watched him swallow, his Adam's apple bobbing in his throat. He nodded, but this time he had no words for her. They closed the doors to their rooms at the same time.

This time, there was no doubt in Aurora's mind about whether Michael felt the same way. His eyes had betrayed him—in the same way that her whole body stood at attention in his presence.

Aurora thought of David and the kids for a fleeting moment, but Michael filled the bulk of her thoughts. What had gotten into her? What were these feelings of abandon, as if the past fifteen years had been nothing more than a blip on the timeline of her life? Hadn't the makings of a life: marriage, the births and raising of her children, making a home for all of them, and the continued upward trajectory of her and David's careers amounted to more?

How could she feel so untethered to her family? That she could bet her future on a stranger?

❖ ❖ ❖

On the second last day of the retreat, Aurora reviewed what she had written. She was shocked to find that she'd written thirty thousand words in the span of a few days. She'd never been a fast writer, and quick writing had never netted her quality work. As she read over the story, she found herself glued to her own words. Something had cracked wide open within her, allowing her to pour her own machinations onto the page—a real-life vessel for her fiction. She knew the climax hadn't happened yet—it was the one piece of the puzzle she couldn't yet figure out. The problem with romance writing was that readers expected happily ever after. A tidy resolution where the main characters triumphed over all things.

That night the retreatants were invited to showcase their work during an evening open house. Artists would have some of their work on display in the great room. There would be an open mic for the writers interested in reading. Aurora didn't like to participate, but the opportunity to see Michael brought her out of her room.

She dressed in her best clothes, which wasn't saying much considering she'd expected to stay in her room most of the week. She'd brought yoga pants and sweats, mostly. She settled on the yoga pants that compressed her skin the most and made her the curviest. She added a pink blouse that brought colour to her face and coupled the outfit with larger earrings that might elevate her look. She was careful to apply her makeup, and wished she'd brought a fragrance with her. Instead, she applied extra layers of anti-perspirant, hoping that the baby powder scent came off differently to anyone near her.

Satisfied with her efforts, Aurora made her way to the great room and was surprised to see Michael already there, about to step in front of the microphone for his reading. Their eyes caught again, and they waved at one another as old friends might. She took the nearest seat. Michael cleared his throat and launched into the reading of his poetry.

Aurora hung on his every word. His poem was passionate, vulnerable. It touched her. She felt tears prick her eyelids. She wondered how she'd ever married a man like David when there were men like Michael who talked in assonance, consonance, metaphor, and meter. In sonnets and villanelles. In lyrical forms that tore hearts out from chests and left one writhing for more of the music and pain of something so beautiful.

She was entranced, changed. When he finished his poem, he thanked the small crowd and headed in Aurora's direction. She immediately panicked, unsure how she could keep from him any longer. She stood and headed toward the elevator, hoping she could get herself inside and safely enclosed in her room again before Michael neared.

She pressed the button for the elevator furiously, hoping it would move faster. She could hear Michael's footsteps.

"Aurora!" He quickened his pace. She launched herself into the elevator as soon as the door opened and began pressing the button to her floor. She thought she might pass out from the way her heart was beating, from how ragged her breath was.

"Where are you off to?" Michael's arm stopped the door from closing.

Aurora stared at him blankly, her chest heaved.

"Are you okay?!" Michael's eyes were wide.

Aurora nodded.

He stepped closer to her. She could feel the heat radiating off him and the musky smell of his aftershave. She stepped back until she hit the elevator wall. The door shut behind them, closing them off from all other sound.

Their eyes locked again. Aurora took one step back toward him. Her chest lightly brushed his sweater. He pressed his hand on the elevator wall beside her ear and brushed back the hair that fell into her eyes with his other hand. Aurora held her breath. She stared at his full lips, placed a shaking hand against the back of his neck, and pulled his mouth toward hers. Their tongues sought out one another; their lips pressed hard. It was the most passionate kiss she'd had in her life, and his hands shifting to her body made her feel more desirable than she'd ever felt. They kissed with fury. He paused to let her catch her breath and kissed her earlobe and the nape of her neck. His hands travelled over her breasts. She started tugging at his pants—she'd never wanted anyone so badly.

The elevator dinged with the arrival of their floor. Before Michael could press a button to buy them more time, the door slid open. The two of them stopped. Aurora smoothed her hair and her shirt. Michael adjusted his pants and coughed lightly.

There was no one waiting. Michael took her by the hand. They stopped in front of both doors to their rooms. He looked at her to see which room they would use. Aurora felt dizzy, drunk. She'd lost all sense of orientation after kissing Michael. She knew she'd have the best sex of her life if they put themselves behind one of these doors. She might even find a better match for her—the love of her life—if she'd give them a chance.

She could feel his racing heart pulsing through his fingers, laced into hers. His eyes were bright. He bit the corner of his lip, waiting. Aurora shook herself from his grasp. The energy discharged from them.

"I'm sorry, I can't," Aurora's voice sounded strangled. She wasn't sure if she meant it. "You're great, but…"

His face fell.

Aurora turned on her heel and opened and shut the door behind her before she dared another minute of time with him. She leaned against the door again. After several minutes, she still heard nothing. She knew he was still standing in the hallway, shell-shocked. Tears sprang from her eyes. She wiped them in quick succession, but they still blurred her vision. Her hands shook uncontrollably. She felt caged in this stifling room with its plain walls. It wasn't a retreat to her now, but a prison cell for her sins. She began throwing her things into her suitcase, desperate to leave as soon as she could.

When the last of her things were packed, Aurora opened her door as quietly as she could. Thankfully, there was no one in the hall. She didn't want Michael to come and find her. It was better this way. She tiptoed down the hallway to the elevator and breathed deeply when she successfully made it to her car. It would be after midnight before she got home. She didn't like driving on the highway after dark, but the thought of staying another night was impossible. All she could think of was getting home to her safe life with David and the kids. She fumbled for her cell phone and turned it on, hoping for another stream of messages from her family. This time, the phone stayed quiet. They hadn't sent another text message after her last one. Aurora swallowed, her throat constricting. What had she done?

I'm coming home. See you soon. Aurora texted. How long would it take David to respond?

Aurora drove out of the parking lot of the Wellspring Creative Retreat Centre. She'd come hoping to gain real ground on this next book and she had. But at what cost? And how could she finish the book? Romance writing relied on happy endings, on couples triumphing over challenge. The couple always found their way to one another at the end.

Just as Aurora merged onto the highway, her cell phone rang. She pulled over to the shoulder of the road. It was David. She pressed the talk button and held the phone to her ear with her trembling fingers.

"Aurora? What's wrong? Why are you coming home?" David sounded frantic. "Tell me you're okay?"

Aurora smiled; her face was bathed in tears. David's voice sounded so good to her ears, so comforting and warm.

"I'm fine," Aurora choked.

"Are you *crying*?" David's words dripped with worry. "Honey, what's going on? Talk to me!"

Aurora couldn't speak. She just wanted to keep listening to his voice. After a few beats of silence, she took a deep breath.

"I'm okay," she managed, though they both knew she was not.

"Are you sure you should be driving this late at night?" The September sun had already set. Soon it would be dark. David knew she didn't like driving at this time. "Why don't I come and get you?"

Aurora smiled again, knowing that David would indeed drive four hours to get her and drive her back home if she wanted.

"I'll be okay. I just want to come home," Aurora said. "I miss you guys." She squeezed her eyes shut and tried to picture David in his lounge pants, his legs crossed beneath him on the couch talking to her. Instead, Michael's eyes kept flashing through.

"I just want to come home," she repeated, as if trying to convince herself. She could still turn the car around. She stared down at her left hand gripping the steering wheel. She'd squeezed the blood from it, her knuckles white.

"Okay, honey. If at any point you feel like you need me, just call. I'll come as soon as I can."

Aurora nodded through her tears, even though she knew David could not see her.

"Will do."

"Aurora?" David said. "I love you." His voice was like a warm hug, a soothing balm.

They hung up and Aurora turned back onto the road. The sky was about to cloak the landscape in darkness. She thought of Michael's hands on her and his mouth against hers. She'd never forget the moment; it would thrill her and stay locked within her forever. But she knew she'd done the right thing. She had David and the girls waiting for her at home.

It wasn't the story she thought she'd tell, but she could feel it's resolution forming in her mind. That was the thing about writing romance. Sometimes tropes had to be spun on their heads and re-imagined for the narrative to be successful. *Maybe*, she thought, *the right ending would find a way to the story after all.*

Crash

Joel and Brad were on the last twelve-hour night shift of their four-day rotation on the ambulance when the call came in. Brad was driving, something he insisted on, despite Joel's opinion that he was a terrible driver. It was always Brad's way. He'd made it clear on their first day as partners that he wasn't about to start listening to some punk kid new to the job—even though Joel had been a paramedic for ten years. They'd been working together for only four months and already Joel was ready for a partner change.

"Open road, no witnesses. Drunk driver?" Brad said aloud. "Kids racing?"

Joel didn't answer. If he took a guess about it, Brad would rib him all night if he got it wrong. He was like that. Joel rubbed his eyes and stared at the inky sky as they drove. It was three in the morning. His stomach gnawed at him—this was the third shift in a row that they'd been too busy to get a lunch break. He'd been counting down the hours until the end of shift, eager to collapse into his bed away from the dark recesses of the world. An accident like this might put them into overtime. Joel hoped another unit made it to the scene before them; with any luck, they'd be diverted before they got there.

"Shit," Brad muttered as they approached the accident. There were no other ambulances there. Just police and fire—the lights from their response vehicles illuminating the road and surrounding embankments in red and blue. "We're the first ones."

Joel shifted uncomfortably in his seat. Realizing he'd been thinking the same thoughts as Brad felt like a poison on his tongue. No way did Joel want to be a washed-up cynic like him. Brad steered them closer and the two of them pulled on their gloves before exiting the ambulance.

"What do we have here?" Brad strode into the middle of the scene as though he expected crowds to part for him. Joel had initially pegged it as confidence but had since deemed it arrogance. Joel carried the jump kit, as always, and approached the scene with his eyes first.

Snowflakes dripped from the sky in sheets of white crystal, disappearing once they made impact with the grey pavement. The air was crisp and still, almost eerie. That's what Joel really noticed—how quiet it was. His eyes surveyed the accident, the two vehicles almost unrecognizable—a white minivan and what looked like a silver luxury vehicle—what model, Joel couldn't tell. It looked like God had put the two vehicles in His hands and shaken them like dice, pieces strewn across the road in a gut-wrenching puzzle. He scanned again for people inside the vehicles but saw none. A firefighter pointed and Joel looped around the car. A tight-knit circle of firefighters kneeled around a figure on the ground. A couple of police officers surrounded them to maintain scene control. As Joel and Brad approached, the firefighters scooted back to give them room.

"How many?" Brad asked.

"Two injured." A firefighter responded. He pointed to another person at the end of the freeway who was also being attended to. "A female, thirties. Unconscious and breathing but unable to provide any information. Leg fracture for sure."

"And this one?"

"Male, forties. Driver of the Lexus. Conscious, breathing, suspected internal injuries. Blood pressure 132/90. HR 92. Sats are good."

Brad nodded. "You take this one," he directed Joel, before heading towards the woman.

"One fatality," the firefighter added. Joel and Brad's heads spun around the scene. An officer stood by a shape not much bigger than a suitcase—a sheet draped completely over it. The figure was small. Either the patient had no legs or…

He knew without getting any closer that it was a child.

Joel could feel the veins in his neck straining against his skin. This was the rotten underbelly of the job. The kind of call that would stick with you: the smell of the air, the way the November wind prickled your cheeks, the exact location of the accident, the victim's vacant eyes and stock-still face.

"She looks to be about six," another officer said. His voice faltered for a moment. No one dealt well with the death of a child. "Mom was driving the minivan. This one was driving the car," he pointed to the man on the ground. "Suspected intoxication."

Joel nodded. He could feel the blood pulsating in his chest, heat rising to his face. Drunks made up a good portion of their call volume. He had little tolerance for drinkers; his own dad had been a drinker. A six-pack down and his dad morphed into a monster— angry, vile, punishing. Joel knew he had to focus on the injuries at hand, not on the reason for the accident, but how could one remain impartial with a child lying dead on the freezing asphalt?

"Nearby homeowners reported hearing the crash from inside their houses. No witnesses to the actual crash though. A semi pulled up to the scene and called 9-1-1."

The driver of the semi had his head in his hands. An officer scribbled in a notebook beside him. Joel felt sorry for the driver; if he'd been the first to discover the victims, this would stay with him. It would keep him from falling asleep at night, haunt him in his dreams. It would follow him every time he drove this stretch of road, an instant replay in the mind. Joel knew. He'd had the experience before: when a woman who was eight months pregnant was thrown from a rolling vehicle into the ditch; when he'd entered an apartment for a wellness check and an old man had died several days earlier, when a woman was decapitated in a snowmobile accident. He knew this child would haunt the poor guy.

Another ambulance pulled up to the scene. The two medics were briefed before tending to the woman, sending Brad back to Joel. Joel wanted to be the one to tend to the woman and leave this guy with the other medics, but it didn't work that way. One didn't pick and choose.

Joel did a Rapid Trauma Assessment from head to toe. He pressed gently on the patient, probing for possible injuries.

"Ow!" The man swatted at Joel and spit at him.

Immediately, the circle of people around the man moved in to restrain him. Joel wiped his face with the back of his hand. It was a hazard of the job—bodily fluids that could carry the threat of serious illness. An officer pulled out a spit sock and placed it over the man's head. The man writhed to avoid it, a fish out of water. Joel studied him as he tried to twist and turn. He wondered if the man knew he'd killed someone. A child no less.

"Go to the truck," Brad said. "Spike two bags of normal saline."

Joel looked up at Brad, perturbed. He was only midway through his assessment. He pretended he didn't hear him and continued. Brad pulled on Joel's shoulder. Irritated, Joel shook him off. But Brad was the senior medic. Joel had no choice but to defer to him.

Joel opened the back door to the ambulance and climbed in. He'd do whatever prep was necessary and they'd get this guy to the hospital and call it a night. His eyes burned. He rubbed them and took a deep breath. *Almost done*, he thought to himself. He prepared the IV supplies and paced back to the patient. The man was now secured C-spine, ready for transport. Brad rose and breezed past Joel.

"I'm not sitting with that guy," Brad laughed. "No, thanks."

What did he mean he wasn't going to sit with him? Brad was just going to leave him with the patient and not provide him the results of his assessment? It wasn't how things worked; whoever was going to sit with the patient in the back should know their vital signs and possible injuries before they hit the road. Brad knew full well what he was doing was wrong. It was his *job* to treat the man. Joel threw up his hands.

"What?" Brad smirked. "This is your attend. I was the one driving, remember?" The driver's side door shut with a distinct thud. Brad wasn't kidding. He was always lazy like that, relying on Joel to do the grunt work. One of the firefighters helped Joel load the man into the back of the unit. Brad was whistling and scrolling through his phone as the two of them got the patient settled in. Joel's fists tightened. His breathing became ragged. He wanted to smash Brad's phone, punch him in the face, even.

Joel remembered once being excited for these types of calls. Paramedicine was running into situations others were running away from. He'd once thrived on the adrenaline of it all—the opportunity to help and play the hero. Good paramedics looked forward to the serious calls; it was a chance to hone your skills and put you at the top of your game. It was all a challenge: heading into the unexpected, sorting things out, diffusing the highest of emotions, reinstating equilibrium for the patients while you ignored the blizzard in your own gut.

"You need to stay still," Joel directed the man. His voice was flat, indifferent. Part of him wanted the man to bust out of the straps, stumble out of the unit, and collapse on the middle of the street. Unfortunately, the five-point harness kept the man contained—a swaddled bundle in flannel. As Brad pulled away from the scene of the accident in the direction of the hospital, the man hollered.

"Driving like a fucking maniac!"

"Trying to kill me here?!"

It wasn't the driving. Riding in the back of an ambulance felt like driving with square tires the way they jostled around in the unit. Joel caught a glimpse of his boots. There were blood spatters and the remnants of vomit from their last two calls. Both patients had been gravely ill. He wondered if each of them would make the night—if they had treated them in time.

"Why are you keeping me here anyway?"

"I have rights! I want a lawyer!"

Joel smirked. *This guy will get a lawyer all right.* The stench of alcohol seeped from his pores.

"I'm filing a complaint. You won't have a job by the end of the night." The man pointed the finger with the pulse oximeter toward Joel's chest.

"Try to remain still, sir," Joel reminded him.

"Give me something, already!"

Brad called back to Joel. "What are you doing to the guy?" It was meant to tease, but Joel wasn't in the mood for Brad's quips.

"Ow! It hurts! You gonna help me or what?"

Joel was helping him. He had started an IV for pain control and fluids, taken his blood pressure, and he was monitoring the man for any changes. The man was stable. At this point, he'd require diagnostic tests at the hospital to pinpoint his injuries.

"Give me some fucking drugs!"

Joel, unphased, listened to the man's lungs with his stethoscope. Snowing the man with Midazolam was tempting. They could continue down the street in peace, the patient sleeping soundly like a baby.

"Hey, you piece of shit! I'm talking to you!"

Joel didn't respond.

"Good for nothing," the man muttered.

Joel stopped. It was this that unnerved him. Those words. At once he was a boy, living on that dusty remote farm, far from any kind of meaningful livelihood that might have saved his father, and far from any neighbours nearby to witness the brutal consequences of his father's dissatisfaction. He was transported to that sweltering summer day, the sun blazing on their little homestead. A day that felt full of promise. He'd rushed to show his dad how neatly he'd organized his tools. It was a favour done to win his approval, but his dad, a 26 deep in vodka, had raged at his tools being moved.

"How will I ever find a goddamn thing," he'd yelled. "You think you can just come in here and touch someone's stuff?" His dad set to ripping everything apart, the ear-piercing clang of metal as each piece landed haphazardly on the garage floor. Eight-year-old Joel had crouched in the corner, his hands held over his ears to try to soften the sound and his jangled nerves. His dad had towered over him, pulling Joel's chin up so their eyes met.

"You," his dad had enunciated the words slowly for emphasis. "Good for nothing."

Joel's chest tightened. He marvelled at how three simple words could have the power to transport him back twenty years. How this man, a stranger, could reduce him back to that helpless, broken little boy. Joel's head spun. He couldn't muster an ounce of empathy for this mouthy drunk knowing his actions had resulted in tragedy. He knew he needed to compartmentalize and set this feeling aside, but he found the feeling gathering steam: absorbing every awful thought he'd had about his useless dad, the death of his mom, his messed-up, lonely childhood. He thought of the dead child's body lying on the road just a few miles away, a consequence of this man's actions, and smiled bitterly. The truth was: Joel wanted this guy to feel every ounce of what he was going through.

He wanted to tell the man what he'd done—how he'd injured a woman and killed a precious child. See if that did something to him. He'd likely not remember, being as drunk as he was. They usually didn't impart that kind of news until the person had sobered up. He *wanted* the man sober. To be gutted by the news. Joel wanted to enunciate every word, slow and sure.

"Got quiet back there. What? Did you lull him to sleep with your riveting personality?" Brad's sarcasm. Joel blinked. He hadn't noticed the sudden silence. He studied the man. His chest was still—no rise or fall of breath. The monitor showed his heart beating much more rapid than it should and Joel knew before he assessed him that the man had stopped breathing.

"Hey, wake up," Joel whispered.

He did a sternum rub with his knuckles. Nothing. A man who was conscious or faking would respond to painful stimuli.

"Did he fall asleep?" Brad called back. It was common for drunk patients to pass out.

Joel's heart thundered in his chest. He knew exactly what he was supposed to do, but he couldn't bring himself to do it.

"Yeah," Joel answered. He'd never lied like this. Never crossed over into this kind of treachery. The ambulance slowed; Joel knew by the low speed and the turns of the unit that they were approaching the hospital grounds.

Joel stared at the dance of lines on the heart monitor. The rhythm was erratic now. It would only be a matter of time before the man's heart gave out. He wondered if he'd last.

When the ambulance finally pulled into the bay, Joel stayed frozen in place.

Brad threw open the back doors of the unit. He took in Joel's pale face, the beads of sweat that fell in thin streams along his cheekbones.

"What's up?" Brad asked, confused. He looked back and forth to Joel and the patient.

"He coded," Joel whispered.

"Holy shit!" Brad leapt inside the unit, checking for a pulse and preparing to do CPR. "Get the bag valve mask. You bag him."

Bile rose in Joel's throat. He watched as Brad stood over the man and started chest compressions. Joel moved robotically. He could barely see straight.

Another ambulance was about to clear from the hospital. Brad called for their help and they worked to unload the stretcher while Brad and Joel continued CPR.

"Let's get him in there."

Joel pressed the bag in a steady rhythm and shuffled through the doors but sweat blurred his vision and stung his eyes. His feet carried him even though he felt like he was floating somewhere above, having an out-of-body experience.

The doctors and nurses were distorted, their voices faint and garbled. He could hear Brad giving them the report and found himself laughing inappropriately. Brad had relinquished care to *him* on scene. *He'd* been the one to do all of the work. Of course, Brad would give the report. He always needed to be the hero. Someone pried Joel's hands off the bag and the stretcher rolled away from him. The man's fate belonged to someone else now.

Joel followed Brad back to the truck to start their paperwork. Once they were seated and belted in, Brad tilted his head to look Joel in the eyes.

"You okay?"

Like Brad cared. The thought of Brad thinking of someone besides himself was another laugh. To Joel, Brad represented how not to practice paramedicine.

"Unit 1256, you're clear to head back to base," the dispatcher's voice crackled through the radio.

"Ten-four," Brad responded. "Unit 1256 is going home!" He put the truck into drive and tore out of the ambulance bay; the obnoxious squeal of tires turned heads.

"Have a great night," the dispatcher added.

Joel didn't speak. He wiped the sweat from his brow and felt a sting. His knuckles were cracked and bleeding from the cold and the constant sanitizing. His body ached. He couldn't wait to get out of the unit. He felt caged, like the walls were closing in on him. He needed to go home, lose himself in a B-movie, maybe pour himself a stiff drink or two to erase the night.

The streets were near deserted. Soon the world would be waking up—most people safe in the knowledge that they'd experience another ordinary day. Joel wasn't even sure what ordinary looked like anymore.

Brad's jaws wouldn't stop moving. All Joel could hear was the constant snap of Brad's gum being tossed within his mouth. Joel switched on the radio, hoping to drown out Brad's incessant chewing. Brad tapped on the steering wheel to the beat of the tune playing, each hit more deliberate as the song reached its crescendo. Joel leaned back on the headrest and shut his eyes. He didn't want to come off like he was difficult by asking for a partner change, but he wasn't sure how much longer he could take working with Brad.

He'd gotten into this profession hoping to make a difference in people's lives. He'd always prided himself on his patient care. Joel was a good medic. He wanted to be partnered with someone who cared about the job as much as he did. *That* would help everything. *Yes*, he thought, *a partner change.*

That's all Joel needed to keep doing the job. He was sure of it.

A Mother's Love

After several months of coaxing, our son Matthew is bringing his girlfriend to Sunday dinner. I'd figured they wouldn't make it very long and dinner would be unnecessary, but the two of them have proved me wrong. So, considering this long-awaited introduction, I've put out the Royal Doulton, the individual salt and pepper shakers for each place setting, the silk runners. I've cooked lamb, which no one in this family really cares for, but I think it makes a good first impression.

I expect that this girl has put forth the same kind of effort, but when Matthew comes through the front door, she's wearing black leggings and a shapeless tunic. They stride into the entry in their running shoes (it's Sunday dinner, remember?) and laugh over the game of football they've just had in the neighbourhood park. Don't even get me started on girls playing football. The girl holds Matthew's hand and stands just behind him as if he needs to provide cover. In his own childhood home!

"Mom," Matthew says politely. He leans into me and kisses my cheek. His stubble needles at my cheeks. He's typically clean shaven. I prefer him that way. I wonder if this girl has influenced him to grow facial hair.

"Bill, they're here! Hello, dear."

"This is Bea," Matthew's mouth stretches wide. (It's pronounced Be-ah. What kind of name is that, anyhow? Beatrice sounds so much more put together, don't you think?) He's smitten, there's no denying it. I note that he does not let go of Beatrice. The girl comes into better view. Her hair drifts out of her ponytail—brown wisps that create a mane around her oval face. Her cheeks are tinged pink, likely from running, and she smiles as she stretches out her hand to me.

My eyes narrow as I take her in. Her hazel eyes regard me under thick lashes. A scared doe. Bill comes up from behind me and shakes Beatrice's hand before I do, so she isn't left with her arm suspended in the air.

"Let's go sit," Matthew says, pulling Bea toward the living room. Bill and I follow them. Matthew sits on one end of the loveseat and Bea sits right next to him, so that there is almost a full seat beside her. They continue to hold hands so tight; I wonder if Matthew's scared that she'll blow away.

"So …" I begin. "Nice to see you both."

"You as well, Mom." Matthew nods.

"It's been a while." I try to sound warm, but it comes out clipped. "You must be busy."

Matthew squeezes Bea's hand. "This girl is the best thing to have happened to me."

They gaze at each other, their eyes bright. My gut drops. I might as well fling myself off a high-rise and career to my end because

I imagine that moment would feel the same as this, but no one notices the danger I'm in. Matthew leans into Bea and kisses her cheek. I find myself touching my own cheek in response—the whisper of my son on my skin.

I think of how many times I've kissed his baby soft cheeks. How, when he was a toddler, I'd blow raspberries in the crook of his neck and shoulder and his tummy. How his belly laughs would make me clutch my own stomach, happy tears pricking my eyelids. His pudgy hands, warm with sweat, would cup my cheeks. The time when I was his everything.

"Dinner is almost ready," I inform them.

I hope Bea likes my cooking. I've been up since five preparing for the meal and scrubbing the house. If I'm supposed to be past caring what people think of me, I've been squarely brought back to those days. Even worse, I'm reminded of my early years on the pageant stage when my mother paraded me around every chance she could—every inch of me up for judgement and score.

"Why don't I get us some drinks?" Bill is jovial. He sees no problem with Matthew dating Bea or anyone else for that matter. I find myself wanting a drink rather badly.

"I'll have a beer, Dad," Matthew answers. "Bea will have one too."

I check to see if Bea reacts to Matthew's choice for her, but she is studying my son's features with pure adoration. Did I mention they met at a bar? That they would never have met without my attempts at matchmaking? To be clear, I did not choose that venue. A bar is not the place to meet the love of your life.

It started off innocently enough when my friend Donna had suggested we have our single children meet. Both came from respectable families, and we were sure they would hit it off. Her daughter, Elizabeth, was a nice girl from the choir. She wasn't the most striking thing, but she was from good stock. She dressed modestly, which, have you seen the styles today? Ripped jeans, midriff baring tops? Good grief. Anyhow, we convinced our children to meet on a blind date, which was no small feat. They agreed to our plan on the condition that they would also set up two of their friends and go on a double date.

Donna and I were sure that our children would hit it off. I was bringing amazing genetics to the table. Matthew is as handsome as they come. He's tall and trim. He has remarkable grey eyes and a ready smile. His dark brown hair is thick and full; there will be no premature balding. His children will be beautiful, even if marred by the subpar looks of their future mother.

We guessed at what would be the spark to capture each other's interest: Elizabeth's singing voice that hit like a direct soundtrack from heaven itself? Or Matthew's multiple years as a camp counsellor at bible camp? A young man that devoted to the word of God at such an impressionable age would surely be a good father someday, no?

It would have done me some good to consider the past of the person I'd married. One was more likely to find Bill riding in the back of a pick-up truck down a grid road with an open beer in his hand at sixteen than at any bible camp. But that's another story. Matthew is different.

Anyhow, imagine my surprise when I heard that Matthew ended up leaving the date with Beatrice (Bea, I mean, really?) and Elizabeth ended up leaving with the other guy. For all our pre-planning, Matthew decided to date Beatrice instead. I was instantly curious by this stand-in who captured my son's eye. Who wouldn't be?

Bill hands the kids their drinks.

"Would you like a glass? Bill, get them glasses. They don't want to drink out of the bottle."

"Mom, we're good," Matthew says, waving his hand at me to stop.

I watch as Bea takes a swig as large as Matthew's and swallows it effortlessly.

We sit in an uncomfortable silence. I want Bill to initiate the conversation but he's content to sit quietly, nursing his beer. Matthew reaches for the remote and flicks on the TV. I clear my throat and raise my eyebrows at him. He catches my displeasure but doesn't shut it off.

"So, Beatrice," I say. "Are you going to school? Do you work? We really don't know anything about you."

Bea rubs the top of her beer bottle with the pad of her thumb. Her fingers start tugging at the label, leaving tiny bits of foil on her lap.

"I'm interested in holistic medicine. I'm currently working toward being a naturopath." She speaks so softly I find myself craning forward. When I hear the words, I choke on my drink and pass it off as accidental. Bea looks down and sees the mess she's created on her lap. She works quickly to scoop up the torn pieces, but they are damp from the condensation on the bottle, and they stick in wet clumps.

The oven timer sounds, signalling dinner. "Could everyone please take a seat? I'll bring the dishes in."

Matthew stands and places his hand gently on Bea's back to guide her to the dinner table. He pulls out a chair for her and helps get her seated. I flush, pleased that my son is being a gentleman. I've set Matthew's place setting directly across from her, so that the four of us are seated in a symmetrical way.

When I bring out the steaming dishes—a watercress soup, garlic mashed potatoes, roasted asparagus, and the braised lamb— Matthew has moved his place setting beside Bea's so he can sit right beside her. Matthew laughs at the dishes and my face flames.

"We couldn't have just ordered pizza or something?"

"What's so funny?" I demand.

"This just seems like… a little much."

"Your mother spent a lot of time on this," Bill pipes in.

"But we don't even like this stuff," Matthew says. Bea shifts uncomfortably in her seat.

"This is beautiful, Mrs. Johnson." Bea glances at the dishes.

"Thank you, Bea." I am pleased that at least one person appreciates my efforts.

I scoop potatoes onto my plate and wait to pass the bowl to Matthew. He and Bea are leaning toward one another, whispering. I wait for them to notice me, but Matthew pats Bea's knee as if to reassure her.

"Mom, what's in the potatoes? Is there milk in them?"

My eyebrows knit together.

"Cream. Why? I always put cream."

"Well, the thing is … Bea is vegan. And gluten-free." Oh, for goodness' sake, of course she is. She probably drinks turmeric shakes and eats charcoal ice cream too.

I mentally dissect each dish and realize that nothing at the table is suitable for this girl. Besides the obvious lamb, every side dish is slathered in butter or cream. I've even tossed the asparagus with a healthy pat of butter. Bea places her fork back on her plate and folds her hands in her lap.

I look over the entire meal. The steam pulses from the tops of the dishes, all carefully seasoned and placed in my holiday dishware. My jaw tightens. The potatoes in my mouth feel like a dry lump that will not be easy to swallow.

"This might have been something to share with me beforehand, Matthew," I say evenly.

He nods. "Yeah, I wasn't thinking. Sorry about that. Bea, I'm especially sorry to you. I'll make sure we stop at that café you like to go to. We can get dinner there."

So, my son has no intention of staying and visiting with his family. Instead, he will leave the meal I've prepared for him and take her for food she can eat. Was he trying to sabotage this dinner?

"Dessert then! It's crème brûlée, and it should be fine. I used almond milk and cornstarch to thicken it."

Bea's shoulders relax and she nods. "That I can have!"

Bill continues chewing his supper. He watches me rise from the table to grab the ramekins. I hand them out, push my dinner aside, and spoon the warm dessert into my mouth. If dessert is all I'll get with Matthew, I will take it.

Bea takes a generous spoonful of the creamy custard and groans at the taste. I smile. Something at this dinner has finally gone right.

❖ ❖ ❖

One week later, after not receiving one call or text from Matthew, I leave a message on his voicemail.

"Hi Matthew. It's your mother. I thought that maybe you and Beatrice could come for dinner again next weekend. We'd love to see you. This time, I'll know exactly what to serve."

To my surprise, Matthew calls back.

"You were sure there wasn't any gluten in the dessert you served?"

"Why?"

"It's just that Beatrice was really sick that night. She wasn't feeling right for days afterward."

"It is flu season," I remind him.

"True. Okay, well, we'll see you Sunday."

The following Sunday, I greet them at the door. This time, I reach for Beatrice and envelop her into a tight hug. If I'm friendly and warm to the terrified girl, they may come around more. She stands wooden, arms at her sides while I hug her. This irritates me. How can she act so standoffish when I'm clearly welcoming her with open arms?

This time, when Bill brings the drinks, I open the conversation with an article I saw in the newspaper about a shortage of family physicians taking new patients. It said that many citizens are without a regular family doctor, relying only on emergency clinics for their medical needs.

"Have you ever thought of being a real doctor?" I ask Beatrice. "It sounds like there is a lot of opportunity here."

Matthew sets down his beer and folds his arms.

"Mom…" he starts.

"No, I mean it. Why be a naturopath when you can be a real doctor and solve some of the problems in your community?"

Bea's eyes are wide. "Mrs. Johnson, naturopaths do just as much healing as medical doctors do. It's a patient-centred approach, but the focus is on finding the root causes of illness instead of just treating symptoms. It goes beyond what a medical doctor does. In fact, many things can be self-healed with the right approaches. And it is done alongside modern medicine."

I swallow my sip of wine, throw back my head and laugh.

"Well, I'm not sure I'd go that far. If you think your little herbs and tinctures will help people, then you just go right ahead. I'm just saying I'll place my faith in a real doctor." I look Matthew in the eye. "I'm surprised you believe in all of this, since you're going to real medical school." I look at Beatrice again. "Matthew has wanted to be a surgeon since he was just a young boy." To have a son this talented is a blessing I still can't quite believe. I don't want to think that Beatrice is dating Matthew for his career path and the solid future it will afford them, but one must wonder when two people are unevenly matched like they are.

"Nobody said I was going to medical school," Matthew interjects.

"Well, of course you are." I shake my head.

"Dad, will you tell her?" Matthew puts his hands up.

"Tell me what, Bill?" I turn to my husband who has shrunk into his seat. He glances down at his beer like it's a life preserver in a mighty typhoon.

"I think I'm going to go to art school."

My laugh turns brittle and high-pitched. Matthew Johnson will *not* be attending art school.

"Me and Bea, we're thinking of opening a healing centre. With holistic services. And I can teach art there." My son's eyes are pleading with me to understand. I think of his cherubic face holding the Fisher Price stethoscope to my chest, pretending to play doctor from the time he could walk. How he'd carry the plastic black medical bag filled with the make-believe medical supplies. I'd clutch at some part of my body and pretend to squeal in pain until he'd "fix" me. And when I'd announce that I was all better and that he'd saved me, he'd beam.

Now, he sits with this strange girl, the two of them practically intertwined on the sofa, telling me he's not going to go to medical school? How could the past twenty years of knowing exactly what my son needs suddenly go up in smoke with the presence of another female?

"We've got news!" Matthew adds, quickly changing the subject. My blood feels like it's coagulating and threatening to freeze in my veins.

"I've asked Bea to marry me, and she said yes!" The two of them hug and kiss. Bill sets down his beer and claps for them. He gives his son a high five and a bear hug. I feel myself pale. I think I am smiling, but the room blurs.

Once again, the oven timer sounds. This time I've made polenta with beans and greens. I'm certain it will meet with Bea and Matthew's approval. I've even crafted another dessert. I direct everyone to the table again while I bring out the dishes. Bill opens a bottle of champagne and pours us each a flute of it for a toast to the newly engaged couple. Matthew and Bea fawn over the meal. Bea is more open and animated over dinner, as though she's finally found a way into the family that feels comfortable.

"Thank you so much, Mrs. Johnson," she gushes. "I'm so touched by all the trouble you went through to make this meal for me."

I nod and sip my wine. Even Matthew and I catch eyes. He winks at me. I'm not sure I've ever seen him so happy.

"Shall we have dessert?" I ask. "It'll just be a minute."

The warm apple cobbler is resting on the stovetop. It is one of Matthew's favourites. The edges are crisp, and the sauce has caramelized. I reach for the can of whipped cream in the refrigerator but then think better of it. I want Bea to know that I'm thinking of her food intolerances. I grab spoons and the pretty crystal dessert bowls that Bill and I received as a wedding present twenty-five years ago. I want to look back on this moment and remember how it meant something.

I set them on the table and return for the cobbler. I raise it to my nose and breathe in the smell of brown sugar, cinnamon, nutmeg, and cloves. I realize there is one thing I forgot to do—one secret I've almost let slip. I take the yellow bin marked "Flour" and tuck it into the cupboard before anyone sees it and asks. The cobbler won't be the same if I make it with something else. Besides, an intolerance won't kill the girl.

With my chin on my hands and bright eyes, I watch my son laugh as he wolfs down his cobbler. I think of him in his highchair, sticky face and hands after dessert, reaching for me. There's nothing purer than a mother's love. One day, Matthew will know how much I love him and the lengths I'd go to for him.

In Sickness
and in Health

In many ways, Floyd wished the cancer had taken her early. This wasn't living. This was an ongoing hell from which Angela had no escape. She wasn't improving, she wasn't getting stronger, her tumours weren't shrinking, there was no good news to be had. Instead of taking her quickly, the cancer decided to draw the process out. Eight months when the doc said it would be four. Floyd deemed himself a reasonable man, but he'd started thinking wild thoughts about this whole journey. About the whys and the hows and when it would all end.

The faintest wisps of air puffed from Angela's pale lips. They were puckered like prunes, with only the slightest pink to them. The warm colour had long drained from her smooth porcelain face. She had a grey pallor to her, like beef gone bad, if human flesh could be compared to such a thing.

The edges of her mouth were mottled with scabs. The rough, flaky exterior of them made Floyd wince as he dipped the edge of the terry washcloth into the bowl of cool water on the nightstand next to the bed. Prescription bottles surrounded the bowl like soldiers standing at attention, ready for battle. He wrung the edge of the cloth out enough to keep it from dripping onto his wife, but wet enough that she'd feel the relief of it on her fevered skin. Or at least he hoped so. Angela hadn't communicated with him for several hours. There were fewer waking moments as the days progressed.

He hoped she'd respond to the damp cloth, but as he stroked her face and mouth gently with it, there was no indication that she was aware of Floyd's touch. He tucked the sheet tighter around her and stood to stretch his own stiff limbs.

Thunder cracked outside and shook the walls of their wartime bungalow. Floyd longed to raise the window and breathe in the sweet, musty smell of first rain in spring, but he didn't want to chance making Angela cold. The booming sounds played on his nerves. His eyelids hung heavy. He rubbed his eyes and blinked to keep himself awake.

Floyd's eyes followed the plastic tubing that led to her urine bag. It was still a murky sludge, the colour of ripe grapefruit. An acrid smell permeated the air around them, the force of her fourth bladder infection keeping Angela listless. Three days of antibiotics hadn't changed a thing. Floyd's fingers curled; blood rushed to his face. He wished he could take all this away from her. She'd always been the better person of the two of them—the softness to his sharp edges, the gentle balm to his natural wariness of the world. She didn't deserve this kind of suffering.

❖ ❖ ❖

A massive Alberta clipper hit the day they received the news. Floyd suited up to shovel after breakfast and had only managed to clear a path to the mailbox and the car before heading inside to check on Angela. She hadn't been feeling well for weeks.

"Dr. Serack called. The biopsy results came back. It's cancer, Floyd," Angela said matter-of-factly, as she wiped toast crumbs from the counter.

Salmon pink polish gleamed from her fingertips, catching the light coming through the kitchen window. The colour was vibrant, pretty—a perfect match for Angela's personality. It could have been any other morning. She wiped the counters with the dishcloth while Floyd stood numb at the front door. He kept focusing on his wife's capable hands. "Dr. Serack says it's stage four. It's metastasized into my bones already. There is an aggressive treatment plan we could try, but I declined."

She acted like they were discussing the weather. Floyd felt his legs wobble underneath him. It was the worst possible scenario in the million scenarios he'd played over in his mind.

"Are you sure? They're not always right about these things. People surprise doctors all the time." They'd discussed forgoing treatment if it was terminal but hearing the diagnosis out loud changed everything.

"Floyd, I want to enjoy my last months with you."

He nodded, but the lump in his throat grew until he felt he was suffocating. He opened his lips but could not speak. Angela dropped the dish cloth and came to him. Her cool hands cupped his face, her thumbs caressed his cheeks. She stood on tiptoes to kiss his nose, and he gripped her. She stayed pressed into him. He breathed in her hair; the peach-scented sable locks tickled his cheek, and he wondered how he'd ever let her go.

"It'll be okay," she whispered. Floyd's body shook. He could feel himself losing control. Angela reached her arms around Floyd's and rubbed his back. Angela was the calm, collected one. He had more fire in him—an Irish temper—and he thought he'd be angry now, but he felt the suffocating weight of sorrow instead. Floyd fell to his knees and hugged the back of his wife's thighs. She leaned over him and cradled his head, his thick blond hair in her hands.

"It's okay, baby," she said. "It's okay."

Floyd wished he were a better man, stronger. He'd never forgive himself for falling apart like this when his wife needed him. He'd replay this moment over in his mind, disgusted with his weakness. Angela deserved more.

The cancer had started in her uterus. After two years of trying to get pregnant, they went to the doctor. They were barely thirty, healthy, and they maintained an active lifestyle. They thought starting a family would come easier. They thought maybe they'd start some testing and be referred to a fertility specialist. The goal was a baby, not a referral to oncology. And now, they'd given her a death sentence.

❖ ❖ ❖

Angela moaned. Floyd bent over her, his face near hers. Her shallow breath smelled sweet to him. She hadn't eaten in two days. It was their anniversary—six years of marriage. He wondered if she knew, but then wondered how she possibly could. She'd been trying to keep track and knew it was close, but she'd barely been awake for more than a few minutes at a time on any given day recently. The days had blurred together.

"Is it our anniversary?" she asked. Floyd's eyes grew wide. He smiled.

"Sure is, my love." He kissed her again, this time on the lips. "Happy anniversary!"

She lit up. "Happy anniversary! Are you getting the video?"

Angela insisted on watching their wedding video every year on their anniversary. Floyd always put up a fuss. He didn't need to watch the video to remember what an incredible day it had been. Now, he wanted to watch it with her everyday if it brought her joy.

"It's ready when you are."

She tried to sit up. Floyd added pillows and pulled her up, so she'd have a better view of the TV across the bed from them. He crawled into bed beside her, and she settled into the crook of his arm, her hand on his chest. He pressed play on the DVD player and waited for the familiar musical introduction before adjusting the volume.

He switched back and forth between watching the guests shuffle into the church and his wife's fixated gaze on the TV. He had to smile at her delight. She always looked at it as if she were watching it for the first time, but he was sure she knew every frame.

Floyd watched his younger self shuffle his feet at the altar. He remembered the nerves he felt as the organ music played with greater intensity, signalling the entrance of his bride. He also remembered the instant calm he felt when their eyes met. Her cascading curls, the simple white satin that hugged her curves. She wore white roses in her hair to match the small bouquet she carried. She shook her hips as she got closer and pointed at him before reaching him, deliberately choosing him in front of everyone. The guests chuckled at her exuberance, her natural *joie de vivre*.

"I, Floyd Matthew Murphy, take you, Angela May Pearson, for my lawful wife, to have and to hold from this day forward, for better, for worse, for richer, for poorer, in sickness and in health, until death do us part."

Angela wiped tears from her eyes watching their younger selves.

"Did you know I knew I'd marry you just weeks after we started dating?" Floyd said.

Angela's eyes grew wide. "You mean to tell me you made me wait three whole years when you already knew you wanted to marry me?"

"It didn't mean I was ready just then," Floyd laughed. Still, he regretted the delay now. It felt like time that they'd lost somehow. He'd planned on raising children with this woman, travelling, growing old together. That's what they'd vowed. He hadn't gone back on those vows. He hadn't ever reconsidered their decision. If anything, his love had grown.

The screen flashed to their reception, as the two of them strode through the cheering crowd to take their place at the head table. Guests started clinking their glasses. They kissed passionately and the cheering got louder. Floyd smiled. Angela had fallen back asleep. He muted the video but left it running in case she woke up again. He turned fully toward her and watched her chest fall and rise. She looked peaceful. He thought maybe her fever had broken, but when he touched the skin on her arm, it was far warmer than he expected.

"Floyd?" She called for him, her voice sounded weak but determined.

"I'm here, baby," Floyd told her. He gripped her slight hand in his and kissed the top of it. Her eyes fluttered open at the sound of his voice. "It's time," she said.

"No, Ang. Not yet," Floyd said. There he was, fighting against it. Again. He didn't want to let go. Didn't want to learn how to live without her. His cowardice shamed him. Of all the days, why today? The day that brought them together in holy union, to become the day she's taken away?

"We made a commitment, in sickness and in health," she reminded him. "And you committed to helping me with this when it was time."

He swallowed. He had and he wondered why he'd agreed to such a plan.

"You might feel a whole lot better once the infection is gone."

"You and I both know how I'll feel. The infection barely matters." It was only a partial truth. An untreated infection could be the thing to ultimately take her life, but she had no plans to die that way.

"Just like we said. Except I have another request." Angela's voice was light. How she could remain so calm and content shocked him. He felt like he was being pulled down into quicksand, his body heavy and tired. He felt like he could barely get air.

"What's that?"

"I want to wear my dress."

Floyd paused. She pointed at the TV.

"Your wedding dress?"

She nodded. Her eyes danced. "It was the best day of my life. I want to be buried in it too."

Floyd rubbed his face. It was all moving so fast. He wasn't sure he could follow through with their plan. Angela's face looked youthful and unburdened. Almost excited. He wanted to believe that this was the right choice, that he was doing right by her, but her sudden energy and joy made him leery, unsure. This was not something to second guess yourself about. They'd read in the book the doctor had given them that the dying might have a burst of energy close to death. Was that the same possibility if you were orchestrating your own?

❖ ❖ ❖

"Did you find it?"

Floyd's eyes scanned the new developments in the room upon his return. The bottle of Morphine now flanked the open toiletries bag on the nightstand. Angela had brushed her hair and applied light makeup to her face while he'd been downstairs. He stopped at the sight of her and felt his chest heave. She was gorgeous, as always, and he couldn't imagine walking into their room and not seeing her there anymore.

"I've got it," he said. He spread it out at the base of the bed at her feet.

"Ooh, I can't wait to wear it!" She put her arms out for Floyd to help her out of the bed. She was so small now; it was like lifting a child. "Will you help me?"

"Of course." Floyd could barely get the words out. He had Angela lean against his burly frame while he set the dress at her feet for her to step into. He shimmied the satin over her thin body, noted the goosebumps on her arms despite the heat from her fevered skin. Once he pulled the straps over her shoulders, tears sprang from his eyes. The dress was loose on her now, almost like a kid playing dress-up in their mother's clothes. But she was still beautiful.

"Don't cry, Floyd." Angela said gently. "I'm happy." She nestled into his chest and squeezed him. "You're the best thing that ever happened to me, you know."

Floyd wanted to respond. He wanted to tell her that he'd become a better man since meeting her, that he'd never dreamed marriage would be so good. He wanted to tell her that every good thing in their lives had been because of her and how he had no idea how he'd gotten so lucky. That a man would never find that kind of luck again because there was only one of her. But he did not. Instead, he sobbed. Angela sat back down on the bed.

"I want that barrette in my hair. You know, the gold one. The one your mom gave me."

Floyd fumbled through her jewellery box. He found the vintage clip, likely passed down from one of his grandmas. Floyd wished he'd arranged for fresh roses somehow.

"Can you clip it in?" Angela swept up some of her hair on the left side of her head and gave it a slight twist. Floyd slipped the barrette through her hair and pressed it closed. In that instant, the sun appeared again and lit Angela's face and hair. Floyd caressed his wife's face and studied her.

She sank back down against the pillows. Floyd reached for her legs and swung them easily onto the bed. Her shell pink painted toes peeked out from the bottom of her dress. She was barely a hundred pounds. The dress hung awkwardly on her. Floyd's eyes locked with hers. Even though the rest of her had withered away, her emerald eyes remained bright and full of life.

"Now, just like we discussed. I'm feeling quite nauseous. So, like any good husband, you're going to get me something for that. You're going to go to the car, drive to the pharmacy to pick up my medication and return home."

Floyd nodded, but tears clouded his vision. It was all happening too fast for him. He wanted more time that he couldn't have. Sensing that he needed her, she motioned for him to come closer. He laid beside her and nestled his nose into her cheek. He wanted to keep listening to her voice and feel the softness of her body against his.

He squeezed lavender lotion into his hands and wove them through Angela's. She groaned with pleasure at his touch and at having her hands massaged. He laced his fingers with hers and studied her wedding ring. It wasn't the one he'd wanted to get her. He'd had his eyes on the larger stone until he'd learned the price. Angela didn't seem to mind at all. If she had, she'd never said anything. He'd never seen her take it off in the years they'd been together.

They clung to one another until Angela broke the silence.

"It's time." Two words he'd never hated more.

Floyd wanted to be the man that Angela needed him to be. He wanted to carry forth her wishes and know he'd done the right thing. He wanted to trust in her plan—that this was what she really wanted. Of course, he wanted to end her suffering. This was the biggest act of mercy he could imagine—he just wasn't sure he was strong enough for it.

Floyd took the box of Gravol and pressed the blister pack until a few small pink pills spilled into his hand. Angela had her hand out, smiling.

"I've had a wonderful life, Floyd," she assured him. His hands shook as he passed them to her along with the glass of water on her nightstand. She popped the pills quickly and sipped at the water, coughing. He could tell that she was tired and worn out from the excitement of the afternoon.

"On your way now, Mr. Murphy." Angela motioned for him to go. He leaned down toward her and sobbed into her chest.

"I love you, Angela! I always have. I always will," Floyd's tears wet the front of her gown.

"I love you too. Always have. Always will. See you on the other side," Angela said, but her voice broke, and the ending came out strangled. He didn't want her to be alone, but she'd insisted. Angela pushed him away from her before it was too late. Floyd kissed his fingers and pressed them to her forehead—a final act of love.

He turned to the door, willed his feet to go down the stairs and out to their little blue Honda Civic in the driveway. He knew what would happen next. They'd discussed it a thousand times.

Floyd put the car in reverse, let it roll down the driveway. The world blurred around him. When he couldn't see through his tears, he pulled over to wipe his face with his shirt. When he thought he'd regained his composure, he set the car to drive again and turned off their street. He couldn't believe he was driving at a time like this.

He decided against going to the pharmacy. He wouldn't be able to engage in small talk and pretend that the day was like any other.

Instead, he drove to the park where he proposed. Where their journey to marriage had started. He stayed in the car and stared out at the lush green park. It was glistening from the rain and the return of the sun. He thought of how he'd gotten down on one knee, hoping that Angela would say yes.

It struck him funny how he'd been so nervous, so desperate for her to say yes, as though she might give another answer. Deep down he knew he was getting the better end of the deal. He'd wanted to prove to Angela that he was worthy of being her partner, but he wasn't sure he'd ever truly measured up. After all, here he was sitting in a car while she was-

He couldn't believe he'd let her talk him into leaving the house as she'd requested. It had been stupid. Now she might actually follow through with the plan, and she'd be gone. Had he gone mad? Floyd peeled out of his parking spot and pressed the gas pedal to the floor. He needed to get home, talk to her, see if they couldn't prolong things a little longer. And if not, could he at least be with her? Hold her until the end?

"I'm coming, Angela! I'm coming!" he cried aloud. Floyd veered through traffic, demanding more handling from the car than what was expected of its model. The car was gutless, like him. He pressed the horn and sped through the streets. He turned the corner to their street so quickly, his tires squealed in protest. When he pulled into the driveway, he didn't even close the driver's side door behind him. He ran straight through the front door and up the stairs.

"Angela! Angela!" He called frantically as he bounded through the house. She did not answer. He burst through their doorway, sweaty and breathless. There was his sweet Angela, in her wedding dress, gold barrette in her hair, her hands folded neatly on her abdomen. Her nails and the wedding ring caught the sunlight, reminding him of every time the light had ever caught pieces of his wife and illuminated them for the world to see.

He saw the open bottle of Morphine and knew that she'd followed through. His blood felt coagulated, his limbs stiff. He stumbled toward the bed and grabbed her hands. They were still warm. He watched for the rise and fall of her chest and saw none. He pressed his cheek to hers, waited for the puffs of air to hit his face, but there was nothing. He felt for a pulse. There wasn't one.

"I'm sorry I left you," Floyd cried. His heart felt raw and scraped open—he'd never felt a crushing, searing pain like this before. He scooped her into his arms. His cries were laced with anguish and guilt. He knew she'd wanted to be alone when she did it. She knew he would never have let her follow through if he'd stayed in the room. And he knew it too.

Just then, the sound of clapping caught Floyd's attention. It was the TV. He was sure he'd muted it. Angela must have replayed the wedding video after he'd left. He smiled at the notion of it—that it was him and his bride on their happiest day as the final images Angela had seen.

On screen, Angela's eyes flashed toward the camera. She was smiling wide, the roses in her hair were coming apart and some of the petals had gotten stuck in her curls. Her skin was flushed from wine, dancing, and happiness and she had never looked more beautiful. In a perfect moment, she stuck her tongue out and said, "I love you, Floyd Murphy." Floyd turned around—his suit jacket long removed; the top buttons of his tuxedo shirt open now. In response, he pretended to block the camera lens with his hand and told the cameraman to leave.

"I'm taking her home," Floyd told them, sweeping Angela into his arms. "I've got to get my bride home." The camera filmed them walking away, until they were out of sight.

The video ended abruptly, leaving snow on the screen of the TV.

Dazzle

If Karen hadn't posted on Facebook that she was now an entrepreneur (complete with the hashtags #girlboss and #youcantoo), Pamela might never have found out about it and pressed "like" on her post.

Within a minute, Karen had messaged her directly. "I have the best thing for you! I can't say too much now, but I'll fill you in over java. Saturday?" Pamela was intrigued.

On Saturday, Pamela walked down the street to Karen's house for coffee as planned. As she approached Karen's, she was surprised to see cars parked up and down their street. When Karen answered the door, Pamela noticed a living room full of other faces. "I'm sorry! Did I get the time wrong?"

"You're right on time. Come on in, Pam," Karen said. Pamela wasn't used to just anybody calling her Pam. The furniture in the living room was occupied, so she took a seat on the floor. She smiled politely at the other guests. The postmaster was here, as were some of the girls from the bakery and the local Co-op grocery store. Pamela waved at a few of them and stared at Karen, whose hair was curled in soft ringlets. She looked down at her own white T-shirt and yoga pants. She wished she'd put more effort into her appearance, perhaps chosen a floral print dress.

Karen clasped her hands in front of her as she spoke. "First off, I want to welcome you all here!" She was dressed and accessorized in red; she had even donned red heels that made divots in the carpet when she walked. Large crimson earrings jingled from her ears. "I want to thank you all for coming and supporting me as I launch my new business."

She gestured to the dining room table, which was covered by a pink satin tablecloth. A myriad of shapes protruded from beneath the fabric.

"I can't wait for you to see what I've been working on!" she teased.

Pamela tried to guess what was under the cloth. Karen wasn't particularly crafty, and she didn't have many hobbies either. Mainly, she was best at talking and getting the latest gossip on everyone in town. Pamela hadn't been over since the annual block party barbeque in June.

"This has been a life changing opportunity for me." Karen's voice lowered. "And I think it could be one for you too. You gals are among the first to know about this. You're going to want in. I promise!"

Karen grabbed a corner of the cloth and peeled it back to reveal a table of goods.

"Welcome to Dazzle! A premier lifestyle company that will revolutionize the way you live your life!" Karen motioned to the table, her eyes dancing. "Ladies, we have everything. I can't wait to show you what you've just been granted access to."

The packaging was all uniform—a hot pink with metallic lettering. Pamela listened intently as Karen introduced them to the products. There were meal replacement shakes, essential oils, candles, vitamins, make-up, a full skin care line, and even athletic wear. Karen distributed some of the items for the guests to examine as she spoke. There were nods of approval and awe as Karen shared the information. Each product promised life-changing results.

After two hours of showcasing, the excitement was infectious.

Judy from the bakery put up her hand.

"Yes?" Karen rubbed her palms together.

"You started this company?"

"Not exactly. I'm an independent consultant. That means I run my own business selling Dazzle products. I get to set my own hours, work from home ..." Heads nodded, impressed. "And you lucky ladies can order from the comfort of your home too! And if you order right away, you'll get a 25% discount and a chance to be part of my VIP club."

The women swarmed the table to take a closer look. Pamela watched as catalogues and order forms flew off the table. She clenched her teeth. She wondered how much Karen would be making from this morning. It all looked so easy.

Karen caught eyes with Pamela. "Don't worry," she whispered. "I'll talk to you later. I want you to have this too."

Pamela nodded numbly. Wasn't her therapist just suggesting she take some time out for self-care and wellness? To really focus on taking good care to heal from the divorce?

When the last guest cleared from the house, Karen invited Pamela to sit down at the dining room table. Pamela picked up a small pink box and rubbed her fingertip across the gold-embossed lettering. Dazzle Your Eyes Transformative Eye Cream. She reached for a larger box of Dazzle Your Day Morning Cleanser and felt the weight of it in her hand as she stared at the elegant packaging, then set it back down.

"I want to give you the opportunity to join my team," Karen said. She grabbed Pamela's hands and squeezed them. "You need this, honey. After Joe, and everything."

"I don't have the first clue about selling anything," Pamela admitted. She could feel a ringing in her ears at the thought.

"But that's the thing, the products virtually sell themselves! You saw the women here today. They went bananas over this stuff."

Pamela nodded. They certainly had been more than receptive. Karen really hadn't done much.

"Not only that, but Dazzle provides you with training. It's where I've been driving three nights a week. Up to Saskatoon. You won't believe the following this company is getting. It's important to get in on the ground floor. The sooner you join, the sooner you can introduce everyone to Dazzle and start earning all that extra money!"

"How do I start?" Pamela asked. "Do I send them a resume?"

"No, nothing like that. All you do is pay $125 for a starter kit, and you'll get everything you need to get started."

Pamela's eyes bulged. "You got all of this for $125?"

"Not exactly," Karen said. "I did round out the starter kit with some additional items so I could feature each of the Dazzle collections. But that's optional, of course."

"Money is tight. Even that amount is a stretch right now."

Karen frowned. "Sometimes you need to spend money to make money, Pamela. I really think you could use this right now."

Pamela felt tears prick her eyes. She *did* need something like this. A real opportunity. A chance to turn things around for her and the kids. Ever since she and Joe broke up a year ago, she'd had trouble making ends meet. Her salary as an insurance agent was respectable in their small town, but it just covered expenses. Joe hadn't come through with child support and she was still trying to pay off the legal bill from the divorce. Pamela bit her lip. Karen was right. How could she turn down an opportunity for extra money with this much flexibility?

"Look, they are doing a special recruitment night in Saskatoon this Saturday. It's the official Canadian launch this weekend, with events all over the country. I think you should go."

Pamela nodded. She probably could go to the event. Kyle was eleven now, old enough to stay home alone and look after Abbie. Pamela took the catalogue and recruitment brochure and stood up from the table. She was about to leave when Karen tapped her on the shoulder.

"One more thing," she said. "Are you going to order anything?"

❖ ❖ ❖

The air in the packed convention centre was electric. Pamela studied the people around her, mostly women in their forties. Like her. Many wore shift dresses and carried designer purses, their hair and makeup artfully done. To Pamela, they appeared fresh-faced and lit from within. Pamela wanted that same look. She wanted to exude the kind of confidence she spotted around her. Pamela smoothed the front of her apricot-coloured dress and sat up straighter in her chair. She'd read in the recruitment brochure that to achieve success, one had to look the part. Pamela was careful to choose an outfit that said she was polished but approachable. She wished she'd chosen a dress without sleeves, but she was self-conscious of her flappy upper arms. She hoped she fit in. Had the other women joined for the same reasons she had? Did they desire a better life for their family too?

The lights went out and the crowd gasped. A countdown timer appeared on the giant screen at the front of the room. In ten seconds, the event would begin. Pamela held her breath. Her palms itched from sweat. She could feel it trickle to the base of her spine. Her heartbeat quickened as she watched the number on the screen approach zero. The crowd yelled out the last three numbers: "Three, two, one!"

Spotlights came on, and techno music blasted through the tower speakers perched on each end of the stage. Everyone stood.

"And now, the moment you've all been waiting for … the CEO of Dazzle, Mark Thompson!" Hot pink confetti rained down on them just as the man of the hour appeared on stage. Pamela almost had to cover her ears from the applause. She balanced on her tiptoes to get a better glimpse of him, but she wasn't quite tall enough to see more than the shine off the top of his bald head. His voice, though, was distinctive. He had the charmed voice of a radio announcer, deep and throaty, provocative. Once he got the crowd to settle back in their seats, Pamela finally saw him. He was dressed in a crisp tailored navy suit. He fiddled with his shiny cufflinks as he spoke.

"Thank you, Dazzle family! I am thrilled that you have claimed your rightful places in our company. Endless opportunity awaits! The sky's the limit. The only thing holding you back from living the Dazzle life is YOU!"

A video started on the screen behind him. It featured pictures of airplanes, tropical locations, luxury cars, people relaxing on a beach. The narrator of the video asked, "do you want your life to Dazzle like this? Can you imagine being able to have all of this *and* time for your family, too?" The screen flashed to a mother holding hands with two young girls as they walked along a sunny beach, the surf lapping at their polished toenails.

Pamela's vision blurred. She couldn't imagine being able to take the kids on a hot holiday somewhere. After all they'd been through with the divorce, her kids deserved something like that.

After the presentation, Pamela spotted "It's YOUR time to Dazzle!" and "Be YOUR own boss!" banners hung from the walls and the fronts of the tables. She marched to the nearest recruitment table, fished out her credit card, took a deep breath, and passed it to the woman in hot pink.

❖ ❖ ❖

When Pamela got a parcel notification, she drove to the post office. Elaine, the postmaster, greeted her and had the box ready before Pamela could give her the parcel slip.

"Looks like this is your order!" Elaine winked. "I've been handing these out all day." The box was the same signature hot pink that Dazzle used for its products. Pamela didn't want to tell Elaine that she had not, in fact, purchased anything from Karen's launch. She wasn't sure if she wanted to tell her that she was starting her own business with Dazzle either. Instead, she took the compact box, which was considerably smaller than she expected, with a polite smile.

At home, she felt her pulse quicken as she ripped open the box. Her gut flipped when she realized that the starter kit was far more basic than she thought it would be. She looked again at the starter kit in the brochure and the one that sat in front of her. She looked for the eye cream or the morning cleanser, but there were only a couple of shake samples, a scented candle, travel sized creams, sample lipsticks, and a pair of hot pink leggings with the Dazzle name in metallic silver down the side of the legs. At the bottom of the box was an order form for additional packs one could order to compliment the starter kit.

Pamela remembered Karen's words about spending money to make money. She also reflected on the energy in the room at the recruitment event. The CEO was correct. The only thing standing in the way of starting and succeeding with Dazzle was *her*. She had so little money to get properly outfitted for this new venture. Still, she saw how the women had responded to the products at Karen's launch. She wanted to provide the same experience.

99

Rounding out the starter kit would help.

She read through the training guide multiple times.

"Touch base with all your contacts because as an independent consultant, you have the power to change lives in ways you can't yet see, and you never know what someone needs in their life. Make them feel as though they alone have been chosen."

Pamela made a list of all the stay-at-home moms, teachers, and town staff she knew so she could share this opportunity with them. She also made note of her old friends from high school, her Facebook friend list, and anyone else she thought might be interested.

"Tell them how much you've missed seeing them, how nice it would be to catch up. Schedule a time to meet with them in person. Once you're together, tell them all about this amazing opportunity that's changed your life. Tell them you want this for them too. Make sure you bring your Dazzle products so they can see them for themselves."

That night, Pamela's sister, Leah, called. Sometimes Pamela would let her sister's weekly call go to voicemail. Today, Pamela was eager to share her news.

"Oh, honey, that sounds like a pyramid scheme to me."

"No, it's not like that. It's different. It's selling products. You get paid based on what you sell."

"I don't know. I think you'd be better off getting a second job or something."

Pamela's eyes narrowed. Easy for Leah to say, in her executive house with her doctor husband.

"That would take me away from the kids, and I think they need me more," Pamela said. "This allows me the freedom to set my own hours."

Leah laughed. "Pam, there aren't enough hours in a day to make something like that truly work." This stung Pamela.

"I have to go. Abbie needs help with her homework."

"Find people who will support you in this new endeavour. Remember, you always have the Dazzle team behind you!"

Pamela didn't want her sister's negativity to cloud her decision to join Dazzle. She'd surround herself with others who supported her.

The following week, after Saturday's training session in Saskatoon, Pamela returned to Rosetown feeling buoyed up. She'd met several other consultants who shared their stories of success. They welcomed her and praised her efforts. For the first time in a long time, she felt like she was part of something. In addition, Dazzle had launched a new fundraiser for Mother's Day which would donate 10% of sales to help victims of domestic violence.

Joe had never hit her, but there had been that time he'd blown up over her Christmas spending, and he'd punched a hole in the wall. She'd never been so scared. Being a spokesperson for a company that believed in charity and worthy causes was important. Pamela felt a renewed sense of confidence and decided to visit the women around town. The first stop was Judy at the bakery.

Pamela's mouth watered as she nosed in the parking spot at the front of the bakery. She could smell yeast in the air. She noted the "Help Wanted" sign in the window. She wasn't fit for the early morning shifts that the bakery required. Abbie and Kyle weren't quite old enough to get ready for school on their own, and she wasn't much of a morning person. There was a major risk as well: the temptation of eating baked goods all day, which Pamela knew would not be good for her waistline.

The rich smell of fresh pastry assaulted her senses as she entered the bakery. Judy looked up from the lemon Danish she was setting into the display case.

"Good morning, Pamela!"

"Hi, Judy. Smells heavenly in here." Pamela's eyes scanned the glass cases. She'd surprise the kids with a few long john doughnuts, even though they weren't really in the budget.

"I'll take two coconut long johns, and two chocolate ones with sprinkles, please."

Judy grabbed a bakery box and gingerly placed the doughnuts within.

"So, I started my own Dazzle business!" Pamela started. "I wondered if you'd be interested in the new sales this month?" She started reaching for a flyer to hand her.

Judy's face faltered. "Oh dear, I'm sorry. I've been ordering from Karen."

"No, that's good. Karen was the first."

"I really do like their products. I'm especially fond of the hand cream. Helps with all the cracking I get from washing my hands so often here."

Pamela nodded. "Well, if you ever think of becoming a consultant yourself…"

Judy laughed. "Not for me, I'm afraid. I've got all the work I can handle here. In fact, I'm hiring." Judy pointed to the sign on the door. "If you know someone."

At the post office, Pamela held out the sales flyer to Elaine. She frowned.

"I've been getting all of my products through Karen," Elaine said. Then under her breath, she added, "I'm sorry, Pamela, but it would be weird to switch now."

Pamela nodded. "I understand." She rubbed her arms. Even though Judy and Elaine had been kind in their responses, it was a rejection.

Pamela stopped at the convenience store at the gas station, the library, and the Co-op. Everyone was purchasing from Karen. She wondered if she should go door to door like the Avon ladies her grandmother once talked about, but her spark had been extinguished. She drove home, the doughnut icing melting in the warmth of the May sun. Even her surprise treat didn't go as planned.

As she exited her vehicle, Karen waved from her front lawn.

"Pam! How are you?!" Her tone was overly sweet. Pamela just wanted to get in the house. She waved and hoped that would be enough to appease her neighbour, but Karen started over to her.

"How's Dazzle going?" Karen asked.

"Orders are a little slow," Pamela admitted.

"They'll pick up," Karen said, nodding. "Remember that list. It'll help guide your way.

"I'll tell you the real secret," Karen looked around and then leaned in close. "The real money is in recruitment. Having others join your team."

Pamela swallowed. If she couldn't even get orders from people, how would she recruit them to become consultants?

"Do you have many on your team?"

"My sister, my mother-in-law, my cousin in Regina. And you, of course!" Karen smiled. Pamela noticed she hadn't mentioned any of the women in town. Perhaps there was an opportunity for her to recruit them.

"Consultants get that discount," Karen said. "It's totally worth it. Practically sells itself." Pamela nodded. The box of doughnuts felt soft in her hands.

"Excuse me, I better get inside. I've got a treat for the kids."

"Of course. Well, I'll see you at the Dazzle meeting next week then?"

"Sure will!" Pamela said with false enthusiasm.

The following week, Pamela did the same circuit around town that she'd done the week before. This time, she'd tell them if they placed orders as an Independent Sales Consultant, they'd save more money on the products they'd already grown to love.

"I'm just not sure," Judy said. "I've got enough to manage with the business. We've got new contracts in neighbouring towns. Sorry, Pamela."

"I just signed with Karen last week," Elaine told her. "I'm so excited!"

Agatha and Kelly from the Co-op were considering signing with Karen. She'd offered them an additional 10% and a free bonus pack upon signing. Pamela went home to check her materials. Had she missed the bonus pack? Was she missing information that might sweeten the deal? Pamela decided to call Karen.

"Karen here!" Her bubbly voice came through so loud, Pamela had to distance herself from the receiver.

"Hi Karen, it's Pamela. I'm just wondering … I heard something about a bonus pack upon signing as a Dazzle consultant from

Agatha and Kelly. Did I miss that somehow?"

"Oh, no—that's just something I threw together myself to draw people in. I think it helps having it. You should totally do it too."

Pamela knew she could not afford to create bonus packs for any potential recruitments. She'd barely been able to pay the monthly maintenance fee that came at the end of the month. Karen hadn't mentioned that fee when she signed up. It had been part of the fine print she'd missed.

"Thanks for letting me know. I just wanted to make sure I didn't miss anything."

"You didn't. I think if you invest a bit more, you'll see better results. I saw you only purchased the starter pack. Rounding out the offerings will go a long way. Anyhow, thanks for checking in and being a valued member of our team, Pam." The way she called her Pam made Pamela bristle.

If Karen had already convinced the other women in town that they should sign up with Dazzle, what did that mean for her? She had little in the way of extended family. She was closest to her sister, and that conversation had gone sideways. They hadn't spoken since. Should she try again?

Pamela studied the list of potential customers she'd made. She thought of Mrs. Hanes, her children's preschool teacher. She'd always been a pleasant woman. In fact, she seemed to take a special interest in Pamela each time her children were in her class. It had been years since they'd last seen one another, but perhaps she'd be interested. Pamela scrolled through her email contacts and found her email address. She wondered if it was still current. She wrote a lengthy note explaining her new venture and what Dazzle provided, along with a link to the product catalogue. Pressing "SEND" was easier than soliciting sales face to face. Maybe this would be the way she'd go about it.

The following week, Leah called. Pamela was quiet on the phone as she listened to her sister prattle on about a trip they were taking to the Dominican Republic, how they'd received terrible service at the resort they went to last time and how it better not happen again. Pamela wasn't in the mood.

"Pam, are you there? Why aren't you talking?"

"I'm here," Pamela said.

"You're not mad at me for that stupid Dazzle thing, are you? Tell me you're not still doing that garbage?"

Pamela wanted to say she was remarkably successful, that it had changed her life. She wanted to tell Leah about her own tropical trip, the kind promised to her in the video at the Dazzle recruitment event.

"I am."

"Oh, for goodness' sake, Pamela. Walk away. Really. Before you get any deeper in this."

"Others may be jealous of your success. You may encounter negative feedback. Remember that you are part of a unique team designed to live a life others might not be ready for..."

She'd have to rely on her Dazzle team to get through the sticky parts. They'd know how to handle the people who didn't even want to listen. Pamela heard a notification on her computer. It was an email from Dazzle, congratulating her on her first order. She fumbled to open it and scan it, while her sister kept talking about all the reasons why Pamela should quit.

Mrs. Hanes had placed a five-hundred-dollar order! She'd even included a congratulatory message in the notes section. Pamela felt tears gather in her eyes, clouding her vision. This would help to change everything!

"Leah, I have to go. Someone just ordered another $500 in product. Work awaits." She hung up before Leah could comment.

Pamela re-read the email to make sure she hadn't dreamed it. She clapped her hands and paraded in a circle. Abbie came through the room, with her earbuds in her ears. She saw her mother's face lit up and took one out.

"What's going on, Mom?"

"Oh, just the best day ever," Pamela said. Her eyes danced. "How do you feel about Hawaii?"

Abbie's eyes widened. "Let's go!"

Pamela laughed. "I hope so, baby. Soon, I hope." She kissed her daughter's forehead tenderly and mussed her hair. Abbie wriggled out from her mom and placed the earbud back in.

"Become aware of any lifestyle or health concerns of the people around you. Dazzle can provide the solution! You have the power to change lives!"

Pamela debated calling Karen with the good news, then decided against it. This was one win she wanted to keep all to herself.

Two weeks later, Mrs. Hanes phoned Pamela directly.

"I'm wondering if you could help me, dear. I received my products from Dazzle, but you see, I'm having a bit of trouble with the age-reversing cream."

"Oh no! What seems to be the problem?"

"Well, it seems I'm having an allergic reaction to it."

Pamela frowned. She rummaged through the burgeoning binder that contained all the information given to her about Dazzle. "If I remember correctly, it's all hypoallergenic. Do you tend to react easily to things on your skin?"

"No, dear. This has never happened before. Can I send you a picture?"

Pamela waited for Mrs. Hanes' text to come through. When the picture popped up on her phone, Pamela's hand flew to her mouth. Spread across the woman's face were deep red blotches and angry, oozing blisters. This was a serious reaction.

"I just found the ingredient listing. It says here that everything is natural and hypoallergenic. I wonder what could have caused this. You're sure you haven't used anything else new on your face?"

"No, dear. I'm afraid this is the only thing. I'm wondering if I can get a refund?"

"Of course, Mrs. Hanes. Without question. I will work to file that for you right away. I'm so sorry this has happened to you. Have you had a chance to try out the other things yet? I'm sure you'll be thrilled with them. Dazzle is incredible quality."

Mrs. Hanes laughed politely. "Not yet. I hope they go better than this one did."

Pamela would have to call Karen. She'd never processed a return before. She dialed Karen's number and waited for her cheery greeting.

"Pam! So nice to hear from you!" Again, Pamela had to distance herself from the receiver.

"I need help processing a return."

"Ooh. A return. Gee …" There was an awkward pause.

"What? Is there a problem?"

"Well, the thing is, Dazzle's products are fully guaranteed."

"Okay … great. Right?"

"Well, they are guaranteed as far as the company is concerned. If you should need to file a return you absolutely can, but the return must come from the consultant."

"No problem. I'm more than happy to process the return," Pamela said.

"It would come out of your pocket," Karen added.

"My pocket? Why on earth would it come from mine? The lady had an allergic reaction. She's broken out in blisters all over her face!"

"Dazzle's products are hypoallergenic and natural. Are you sure it was a Dazzle product that caused this?"

"Yes, I'm sure," Pamela said through clenched teeth.

"The re-stocking fee that Dazzle charges is 75% of the purchase price, plus you get a sting on your consultant record for every return made. It's better to just pay for the loss yourself."

Pamela's jaw hung open. How did she not know this? She could feel a tightening vise-like grip on her abdomen. How was one ever supposed to make money at this? Maybe Leah had been right. She might be better off getting a second job. Maybe Judy could hire her part-time to help with the additional contracts at the bakery. What was a few hours added to the start of your day if it meant helping your family?

"Don't worry. You'll get the hang of this soon, I promise. Just stay the course and follow the Dazzle directives. I just got promoted to their Diamond status for sales in May!"

"Congratulations," Pamela said, her voice getting smaller. She wanted to tell Karen that of course she had; she had taken all the possible customers within a 100-kilometre radius of them.

That afternoon, Pamela drove to the bakery. She figured it was time to talk to Judy and see if she could pick up some hours there. At least she'd see a regular paycheck.

When she pulled up, she noticed there was no longer a "Help Wanted" sign in the window.

"Pamela!" Judy greeted her warmly inside the bakery. "What can I get for you today?"

Pamela glanced at the pastries, the doughnuts, the sausage rolls, and the fresh loaves of bread. Maybe there'd be a discount on unsold food for the employees.

"Actually, Judy, I'm here about a job."

"Karen's niece, Amy, has joined us. I hired her just last week."

Pamela bit her lip to keep from laughing, but an unstable snicker escaped her mouth.

"Do you think you could use more help? Just until you get a handle on what these extra contracts entail?" If she gave her a chance, Pamela would work so hard that Judy would have no choice but to keep her on.

"I didn't know you were looking for a job! What about Dazzle?"

"I'm still working with Dazzle, it's just..." Pamela felt her lower lip tremble. "I could use a bit extra..."

"I'm sorry, Pamela. I can't. But if Amy doesn't work out..."

Pamela walked back to her car and slumped into the driver's seat with her forehead on the steering wheel.

I'm finished with Dazzle, she thought. *I'm going to go home and tell Karen that I'm done. She'll be down a team member.*

Then she felt something hot growing within her belly, a fierce anger that bubbled and boosted her resolve. She was not going to be duped by Dazzle and all their sales talk. She'd find another way to make money to take the kids on a trip. She didn't know how yet, but she'd get to looking more seriously once she'd terminated her contract with Dazzle.

As Pamela approached her street, she noticed a pink van with the Dazzle logo parked between their houses. *I wonder what else Karen has won,* she thought bitterly. Karen was standing in her driveway, talking to a team of people in Dazzle's signature pink. She was dressed in all red again, with the same heels she'd worn the morning of her Dazzle launch. Karen waved frantically and Pamela watched the group jog toward her car as she pulled into her driveway, with Karen leading the pack. Pamela exited the car. She knew it was too late, that she couldn't just enter the house and pretend she hadn't seen them. Karen's heels clacked as she rushed toward Pamela.

"Pam! Pam! Come here!" She motioned for Pamela to come closer to the van, the red plastic bracelets on her wrist spinning from the brisk movement. Pamela approached reluctantly. Embroidered on the shirt of each Dazzle representative was the gold Dazzle logo. It glinted in the sun. Pamela even recognized a couple of the representatives from the Saturday meetings.

"Pamela! Just who we wanted to see!" A woman approached with a gold sash and placed it over her before she could protest. Another placed a bouquet of roses in her hands.

Two others held a large placard that read: "Congratulations on achieving Gold status!"

"This is for me?" Pamela looked from face to face, trying to take it all in.

Her children were now standing at the doorway, watching the scene unfold. They clapped for her.

"It sure is! We want to congratulate you on a terrific month, reaching $500 in sales! You have dazzled us all!"

Someone shoved a large pink gift bag into her other hand. Pamela's fingers fumbled with the handle. She took a glance inside and saw what had to be hundreds of dollars' worth of merchandise. Maybe this would be the way to help her sales. Karen had been saying how much those extra items helped.

"Thanks for being on my team," Karen smiled, teeth glinting in the sun. Pamela could feel the adoring eyes of the representatives on her. They came toward her for hugs and Pamela felt tears welling up again. "See? I knew you'd love this," Karen leaned in.

"Stay the course! It only takes ONE sale or recruitment to change EVERYTHING."

Pamela thought of the video she'd seen at the recruitment event. She could do this. She'd just achieved Gold status. With a few more sales, perhaps she'd reach Diamond status like Karen had. That trip might come sooner than she expected. She pictured herself posing confidently on a beach, her children clad in swimsuits dipping in and out of the ocean, and palm trees swaying gently in the breeze. She imagined her chin high, the warm sun kissing her face. They all deserved something like this and now, it had never been closer. If she truly invested in herself for once and severed ties with those who doubted her, she really could change everything. All she had to do was follow the steps.

Thief

"Martin Thompson? This is Constable Lee Swain. We need you to come down to the Safeway to pick up your wife."

"Eleanor? What's happened?" The colour drained from Martin's face. "Is she okay?" She'd been fine when he'd dropped her off to shop while he went home to let the dog out.

"You need to get down here immediately."

"I'll be right there!" Martin had barely finished his sentence before ending the call.

He drove their Buick as though it were a Ferrari through the sleepy suburban streets of Saskatoon. He hadn't even changed from church; his sole-worn spit-shined leather oxfords kept slipping on the gas pedal as his foot, frantic, pressed the car for more. Countless scenarios blazed through his mind. What on earth could have taken place? Eleanor must be terrified, he thought, all alone at the store. She'd always been uncomfortable around police officers—jittery—even though she had nothing to hide.

At the Safeway, the vehicle lurched forward as Martin slammed the brakes. He had barely set the car to park when he noticed a young officer, probably a rookie, standing at the front door. He bolted toward him, his uncertain legs gaining a momentum they hadn't seen for decades.

"Mr. Thompson?"

"Yes! That's me," Martin wheezed. He followed the officer inside. His eyes, wild, scanned the store. His stomach wrenched. The officer led him to a glassed office space next to the customer service desk. After a series of doors, they found Eleanor sitting on a metal chair next to another officer and the store manager.

"Eleanor! Are you okay?" Martin's voice cracked. He felt his heart slow a little when he saw her unharmed. It took a moment for him to realize that she was in handcuffs. His lips trembled.

"Handcuffs? What's going on here?"

"Hello, Mr. Thompson. I'm Joe, the store manager. Our loss prevention officer, Dale, witnessed your wife shoplifting today."

Martin's eyebrows rose. He absorbed the words for a minute, slapped his knee and broke into rolling laughter. The officer and the store manager exchanged glances.

"Did George put you up to this?" Their friend, George, was the manager at a different location. Had he set this up somehow? "George Griffin. The manager at the store on 8th Street. He's a real prankster. But this… this is going too far."

"I'm sorry, sir?" The store manager knit his brows. "This situation is real, I'm afraid."

Martin waited for someone to interject with the real explanation of why he was here, but the room remained silent. Martin's eyes searched the room, certain he was on one of those hidden camera shows; this had to be a prank. There was a gross misunderstanding of some sort. His quiet, sweet wife was no criminal—of that he was sure.

"We found these items in her sweater." The manager pointed to a pack of Energizer batteries and gold foil-wrapped triangles of brie in a red mesh bag. Martin looked at Eleanor. Her steel-grey eyes met his. Her gaze bore into his so deeply, he looked away. For once, he did not know how to read her.

He could see the young officer sizing him up. He was happy he hadn't changed into his regular Sunday lounge wear as he'd planned to before he got the call. He didn't want to come off as a lazy bum who didn't provide for his family. A man who petitioned his wife to steal cheese. Martin had spent thirty years toiling at a job he'd hated. He'd made sure that they were taken care of in their golden years.

"We're prepared to let her go," the officer said. "The manager does not wish to press charges."

"On the condition that she is to stay out of this store," the manager finished. "We'll be posting a notice to look out for her."

Martin nodded numbly as they set Eleanor free. He thought he'd known embarrassment before: when David Pranson pants-ed him on the baseball field in front of their grade eight class, when he'd shit himself in the car on the way to a business meeting, and when his dentures fell out during his retirement speech. Though nothing could have prepared him for the lurch in his gut he felt now.

"That won't be necessary," Martin said. But how could he say that with confidence?

"Mrs. Thompson?" The store manager waited for her to acknowledge what he'd said but Eleanor breezed past them all and exited the store, leaving the men standing in the office and Martin dumbfounded.

❖ ❖ ❖

"Eleanor Grace. You. Did. Not." Martin's teeth ground together. His jawbone danced in his cheek. There was an electricity in the car Eleanor had never experienced before.

"What if I did?" She challenged him.

"How could you? We have more than enough money," his voice trailed off. His hands shook despite his white-knuckle grip on the steering wheel. Eleanor wasn't sure she'd ever seen him so mad.

Didn't Martin understand that this had nothing to do with money? That it was her one thing? The thing that was all hers. It had become a skill—something she was good at. No one suspected a smiling, sweet old lady to steal something and so, she'd gotten away with it many times.

In that regard, she was proud of it. She felt stealthy, unassuming. No one had ever thought much more of her than dependable Eleanor: family cook, competent knitter, excellent housekeeper. Her floors, citrus-scented and gleaming—a source of pride—were so clean that one could eat off them at any time of day. Monkeys could do the kind of work she did. It didn't set her apart from any other housewife on their block. It was *expected* of her.

To Eleanor, her cooking was subpar; Martin was fussy. He was a simple meat and potatoes kind of guy, eschewing any other foods as being too exotic for him. She was bored stiff with boiled potatoes and fried hamburger. She dreamed of cooking in kaleidoscopes of colour and taste—bright cherry red peppers, the warm scent of curry, the lemon-tinged melt of salmon on the tongue.

Their house was the same. A typical 1960s ranch bungalow with an identical layout as almost every other house in the neighbourhood. It was covered in dingy grey stucco. The walls were Eternal White.

116

She dreamed of terracotta tiles in shades of amber and magenta—
not the serviceable beige that Martin insisted on for resale value.
The idea that there was more to her thrilled her.

"We need to talk about this," Martin said through clenched teeth.
Eleanor wanted to drop the whole thing. She'd never get him to
understand. She flicked the radio on, hoping to fill the charged air
with music. Martin pressed the dial to shut it off. They drove in
silence; the steady hum of the motor and the ticking of the signal
lights providing the soundtrack to the ride home.

When they entered their house, Martin went straight to the
basement. He needed some distance from Eleanor. He could hear
her pulling out the frying pan for their Sunday lunch. They were
far past their regular lunch time; he didn't have the appetite for
food now anyhow. Martin sat in the dim rec room; the only light
that filtered in came from the slats of the basement window blind.
He replayed the scene in his mind over and over. What bugged
him most was Eleanor's reaction to it all. She showed no remorse
or embarrassment. In fact, she'd almost looked proud of it.

Martin stared at the photo gallery of their family on the wall; he
glanced at the built-in bookcases that lined the other side of the
room. The mismatched colours on the spines of the titles jumped
out at him. For the first time he saw his home in an entirely new
light. Had those books been purchased? How about the picture
frames? Were the coasters on their coffee table stolen? How long
had this been going on? How much of his life was built by deceit
and missing items from local stores or perhaps someone else's
home?

When Eleanor called him up for lunch, he found her humming
to the country tune on the radio. Her eyes were bright and playful.
Martin's mouth fell open. He was flummoxed. Had she gone
crazy? Was she sick? He'd heard of this kind of thing happening
to people before an Alzheimer's diagnosis. Strange behaviour
caused by some underlying health concern. He would call the
doctor first thing in the morning. Martin slid into the captain's

chair at their dining room table and waited for Eleanor to seat herself before filling his plate.

"Batteries? Cheese cubes?" Martin said between mouthfuls.

Eleanor saw beads of sweat gathering at his temples, threatening to stream down his face.

"Eleanor, you can't be serious." Martin rubbed his eyes.

He blinked a few times as though the answers he wanted might suddenly materialize. Eleanor sat straight in her chair; her legs pointed elegantly to one side. She kept her face blank.

"Have I not always provided for you? Have you not been able to buy whatever you've needed?"

It was true. Although Martin took care of the finances, she knew that they'd never lacked.

"I mean, you could bloody well buy the whole store if you wanted to!"

But these acts of daring had nothing to do with money. It was shocking how easily things could be taken. People were careless with their things. Their attention was easily diverted. Eleanor sat motionless.

"I don't even know if the plate I'm eating on was obtained legally," Martin's voice was bitter. Eleanor considered telling him that the plate was, but his fork wasn't, then thought better of it.

"I think after lunch, we sit down and have a real conversation about this."

"I'm headed to Judy's after lunch. I'm helping with her garage sale, remember?"

Martin choked on his bacon. He coughed and took a quick sip of water to help it down his constricting throat. What if she came home with a trunk load of stuff? Or worse, what if she came home with a wad of cash she didn't have before? Surely, she wouldn't steal from Judy.

"I'll drive you," Martin said. "Maybe Ed will need a hand."

"Ed's gone golfing."

"Well, maybe people need a hand carrying things to their vehicles. I think I should go too."

Eleanor set down her fork. "I'm fine going on my own, Martin."

When lunch was over and she'd cleaned the kitchen, he watched her put her blue sneakers on. He was pleased; he recognized them as the ones they'd purchased at the mall together recently. He knew those ones had been paid for. His stomach clenched again. Martin hated this newfound feeling of distrust.

❖ ❖ ❖

Over at Judy's, Eleanor scrawled details of each purchase into a small, coiled notebook. Judy would be able to scan the list and see what sold and for how much. It would be an easy way to keep track of her sales and reconcile the cash box of which Eleanor was in charge.

"Eleanor, what would I do without you?" Judy cooed at her when the first round of customers headed back toward their cars with their purchases. "So organized."

Judy had a money belt around her pear-shaped hips. From time to time, she handed the build-up of bills to Eleanor for the cash box if she'd been the one to take the sale, so that bills wouldn't tumble from her money belt to the pavement.

119

Eleanor loved the praise from her friend. She'd always envied Judy's carefree life. Judy had gone to university, obtained a degree, travelled extensively and had never married. She had a long-time beau named Ed, but there were no plans for marriage. Everything about her suited Eleanor just fine: her red glasses, her chic blonde bob, her purple face-framing highlights, her Spanish-style house, her eccentric wardrobe, and the lime green colour of her cute compact car. Martin thought Judy's car looked like a booger and that Judy had dreadful hair and dressed like a hippie, but Eleanor paid that no mind.

After reading over her flowery script in the notebook, Eleanor's eyes caught a tangerine-coloured tunic on a clothing rack. The neckline was lined with beads in shimmery turquoise and red. She rose from her seat to examine it closer. She fingered the silky material and marvelled at its originality.

"I bought that in Mexico," Judy said. "Doesn't fit me anymore."

"It's lovely!"

"If you want it, it's yours."

Eleanor slipped it off its hanger. She'd never owned anything like this before.

"Try it on," Judy said.

Eleanor slipped the tunic right over her plain white T-shirt and was pleased to see that it fit well, despite the layer of clothing underneath. She decided to keep the tunic on. She liked the brightness of it and how the sunlight made the beads shimmer. She hoped she looked like Judy, the kind of woman who travelled and lived independently. A woman who took chances.

"How much do you want for this?" Eleanor asked, pointing to the tunic as they packed up the remnants of the sale for the day.

"Don't be silly," Judy said. "I don't know what I would have done without you. I'm just so grateful you were able to help."

❖ ❖ ❖

It was 7:00 p.m. Two hours past their typical suppertime. In forty-five years of marriage, except for special occasions, the only time Eleanor had missed making supper was the night each of their four children had been born. Martin had paced through the kitchen, opened the refrigerator many times, eyeing possibilities. To be honest, he couldn't see what items he could successfully put together to feed himself. Sundays were pot roast, and he had no idea how to cook a roast.

Eleanor had come home an hour earlier wearing God-knows-what—some awful orange looking thing that reminded him of a sparkly pumpkin, a cast-off of Judy's, no doubt. She was practically floating, and it irritated him.

"What's for supper?" Martin said, gruff.

"I don't know," Eleanor fluffed her hair in the hall entry mirror. "You'll figure it out."

Martin's cheeks flushed. His heart picked up pace. "What on earth is going on, Eleanor?"

"I'm going out." Eleanor decided in that moment. She felt like a new woman in the tunic. Emboldened.

"Well, why didn't you say? I'll get my shoes."

"I don't think so, Martin. I'm going to that new Japanese restaurant. I don't think you'd like it."

She was right. Martin had to be careful with what he ate. Whenever he veered from his usual, he often paid for it in the bathroom. He preferred to keep things as they'd always been to limit any upset.

121

Martin watched as she closed the front door behind her and strutted out to the car.

He scratched his head and gazed down at the dog who looked as perplexed as he was.

"Well, boy, I guess we have to fend for ourselves."

Martin combed through the cabinets and the refrigerator once more. He decided on the bran flakes typically reserved for mornings and figured he'd come to no harm by veering from the typical Sunday evening fare just this once.

Eleanor would come home, get whatever was happening out of her system and tomorrow they could go back to the way things were before the Safeway fiasco. A life where his wife was the woman he thought he'd married.

❖ ❖ ❖

Eleanor sat tall and sipped her wine. For the first time in her life, she felt exotic and exciting. She'd never dined alone before. She sampled several dishes knowing there'd be plenty of leftovers to take with her. She thought of Martin at home, knowing he didn't know how to cook. For a brief moment, she wondered what he'd do, and for once, she found that she didn't really care.

She knew that Martin needed her. He'd have no idea how to do laundry, scrub the toilets, deadhead the geraniums when they shrivelled or can the tomatoes and pickles. She loved him, of course, but she'd had enough of catering to his needs without consideration of her own.

When the bill came, Eleanor pulled two folded twenty-dollar bills from her purse. She'd earned that money today and it had netted her a meal she'd enjoyed immensely. Eleanor left a generous tip—something Martin would never do no matter how good the service—and bid the staff a hearty good-bye. She walked slowly to the entrance so that the other patrons might see her stunning tunic. For once, she felt like the woman she'd always wanted to be.

First thing Monday morning, Martin phoned the doctor's office. He told the receptionist that Eleanor was acting strangely, but she couldn't get them in any sooner than the following Monday. Martin took the appointment. He wasn't sure how Eleanor would react, so he'd wait to talk about it later in the week.

On Tuesday, the two of them went to Walmart for groceries. Martin was sour. He hated the big-box store. He missed the elevator music that played through the speakers at the Safeway, the clean and well-labelled aisles. At this Walmart, there was no music. The floors were dirty. The overhead fluorescent lights flickered in places. Neither of them knew where anything was.

Eleanor tried to send Martin to gather a few of the items on the list to speed up the process, but Martin refused to leave her side. He watched her carefully when she bent down or reached up for something. He looked for any bulges in her sweater pockets. He zipped her purse shut and offered to buy items that weren't even on the list.

"Do you want some of those shrimp cakes you like? Or should we get mushrooms with our steak?" Perhaps if he offered her these extras, she wouldn't feel the need to steal something again. Eleanor shot him a death stare. This was not something that would be solved by mushrooms.

On Tuesday night, Eleanor left for the evening for supper and a movie with some of her girlfriends. He was shocked to find out that they'd also gone for a drink afterward. She was usually in bed by nine, so when she tiptoed into the house at eleven like a rebel teenager, she found him pacing, phone in hand, ready to notify the police.

In fact, she'd been finding reasons to be out all week. She'd tell him with little to no notice, and there he'd be, alone in the house and trying to fend for himself. He'd eaten more bran flakes than any grown man should have to eat. His bowels reminded him. If he didn't get Eleanor cooking again soon, he was scared he'd waste away.

On Wednesday, two of their children phoned to check in on them. Martin took the call, of course, since Eleanor was out.

"Nothing new around here," Martin lied to each of them. "We're doing fine. Just fine."

He debated telling their oldest, Claire, that something might be wrong with their mother, but then decided it was best not to worry anybody. They'd know more after the doctor's appointment. Besides, it would invite questions. And what would Martin say? That their mother had a secret life? As a thief?

On Friday, Martin attempted to surprise Eleanor with supper after her Tai Chi class. He seasoned the ground beef with salt and pepper and onion salt. He'd seen Eleanor crack eggs into the meat before, so he added a couple of eggs into the mixture. It felt soft and squishy in his hands, and when he tried to form a solid patty, the meat was so moist, it fell apart in the pan. Smoke billowed from the aluminum. He'd had the heat too high. He remembered that he needed oil, but by then the patties were charred and raw in the middle. When Eleanor walked through the door, she was greeted by an acrid smell and the incessant blare of the smoke alarm. He swatted at the smoke with a tea towel and thought for a moment that he caught her smile.

On Saturday when Martin ran out of underwear and socks, he fashioned a neat pile by the washing machine, but Eleanor paid no attention. He turned a dirty pair inside out and prayed that he'd get to and from the car wash safely. He'd be mortified if he were in an accident and first responders found him in dirty underwear. When Martin realized that Eleanor had no intention of washing the load, he threw the clothes into the drum of the washing machine and added a generous scoop of detergent. He had no idea how the darn thing worked. He looked at the cycle names and said a prayer before pressing a button.

By Sunday, Eleanor looked like she was living her best life while Martin was withdrawn and haggard. The week had taken a toll. When the church service ended, Martin went straight to the car and waited for Eleanor to be done visiting. He noticed the way the sun played off her silver hair as she stood talking. The pink of her dress added a pretty glow to her face. He saw the way her face lit up as she smiled, and then how she threw her head back in a throaty laugh. He caught himself grinning at the sight of her and felt a swell in his heart.

No matter how much they'd been through over the years: job transfers, their parents' illnesses, their first child arriving stillborn, the fire at the family cabin—he'd never stopped loving her. She'd always done so much for him and their family. It was something he'd taken for granted. He'd have to find a way to prove to her how much he loved her. When Eleanor finally made her way to the car, he took her hand and squeezed it, surprising them both.

"We need onions for the pot roast," Eleanor said. It had been a week since she'd been busted and, in that time, so much had changed. Martin drove past the mall where the Safeway was located but braked at the last exit. He steered the Buick to the nearest parking spot.

Eleanor stared at him.

"I can still go in," he reminded her. "Do we need anything else?"

She shook her head. She watched as Martin sauntered away from the car. He stopped and waited for several cars to drive by before deciding that the lane was clear enough to cross. He was always such a cautious man; she knew that could be a good thing. He'd taken really good care of his family over the years.

Eleanor flicked the radio station from News Talk Radio to her preferred country station. She hummed to the music. She watched the people as they entered and exited the store. She wondered what would happen if she stepped foot in there. Did they really have a sign with her profile tacked up to alert the staff? Would police descend upon the place and escort her out? She wasn't about to find out.

When forty-five minutes went by, Eleanor grew worried. Martin was a man who loved efficiency. If it took this long for a bag of onions, Martin would be livid. She shifted in her seat and tried to be patient. When she realized that the entire Sunday morning Top Twenty Countdown had played and Martin still wasn't back, her heart started thrumming inside her chest.

Just then, a patrol car pulled along the fire lane and stopped. A young officer stepped out of the car and made his way inside. Within minutes, her precious Martin was being led, in handcuffs no less, to the patrol car. He squinted from the sunlight. His eyes searched for hers once they'd adjusted. Eleanor fumbled for the car door handle, sure that there was some mistake. Her husband was no criminal, of that, she was sure.

When she ran to his side, faster than she'd done in years, he smiled larger than she'd ever seen him smile.

"Mrs. Thompson?" the young officer said. "Your husband has been arrested for shoplifting."

Eleanor put her hand over her mouth. She met Martin's hazelnut eyes. For once, she didn't know how to read him. In that moment, she had never loved him more.

The Game Isn't Fun Anymore

Clunky wooden shutters around the restaurant's seating area are pulled back from the windows with eye hooks. A soft breeze flows through the screens and kisses my shoulders. The walls are permeated with the smell of oil and deep-fried fare, even during breakfast.

My thumb rubs the lip of my diner mug, but the stains remain—a tan patina from hundreds of people before me. The dimension of time has always thrilled me, or it did when I believed my whole life was still lying ahead. Still, the lines fascinate—the formation of coffee stains as a historical record. How many people have sipped from this same mug? Did anyone sit slouched over their toast, like the bottom had dropped out from under them? Or am I the first?

I glance around the restaurant. A couple takes careful bites of their breakfast. Their sun-spotted hands and creased faces focus on cutting their sausages and they do not make eye contact. My ex-boyfriend Lyle (and ex-coworker now too) and I used to have a game where we'd observe the people around us and invent lives for them. We'd give them dire fates so that we could feel superior; it felt good to imagine that we were the lucky ones. I picture Lyle beside me, will him into being. His dark hair, always unkempt but charming, slides in front of his chestnut eyes.

"Let's play the game," I say in my head. He half-smiles, stares out the diner's open window screen at children on their bikes. "I'll go first."

I turn back to the elderly couple. Their eyes drift in different directions. They bring their forks to their lips and chew with a perfunctory politeness that makes me think of strangers on a first date. At first, my chest aches at the sadness of spending a lifetime with someone and not having anything left to say. Did one of them have an affair? Did they lose a child? Should they have divorced decades ago?

Nothing comes to mind. Imaginary Lyle disappears and I can no longer conjure him beside me. My lips tremble. Somehow this game used to be fun: pre-break-up, pre-job loss, pre-existential crisis. Brutal stories about this couple's life fail me. Their eyes are light and kind, and I decide they keep a content, comfortable silence.

Two young girls enter the restaurant and order ice cream cones, even though it's barely ten in the morning. Their messy ponytails are wiry and windblown. They are barefoot and in purple bathing suits. They aren't much younger than I was last time I was here. The summer I met Melissa.

It is 1990 and I am eleven years old. A record-breaking heatwave creates a heat dome in our yellow nylon tent more suitable for cooking than sleeping, even with the fly off and the screens open to the still air. I want to lay down and read, but my sweaty legs keep getting stuck to the sleeping bags. I decide my only relief will be to head to the beach and dive into the lake.

I pedal down to the beach. I expect to hear laughter and shrieking from the water, but it is strangely quiet, even for mid-afternoon on a Monday. There is a lone orange towel left on the sand. My gaze travels across the landscape. I can't see anyone. I kick off my flip flops and tear off my sweaty T-shirt, happy that no one is around to watch me.

I tiptoe to the edge of the lake and suck in my breath when the water reaches my shins. Despite the August heat, the water feels like daggers against my pale, sweaty skin. I walk knee deep before plunging under water.

"Wow. You didn't waste any time," a voice says, not ten feet from where I come up for air. I whip my head around. I'd been sure that I was alone. A girl stands on the pier with her hands on her hips watching me. She is everything I am not: several inches taller than my compact frame, with a full chest and a perfectly flat stomach that makes her look years older than me. She has a golden mane of naturally curly hair that frames her blue eyes. My own hair is a dirty blonde that hangs limply around my face. Not even the newly added layers give me volume and body. I remain underwater on purpose. My purple Speedo feels dowdy and childish next to her ample cleavage in her white two-piece bathing suit.

"Do you talk?" the girl asks. Her arms are crossed in front of her. Her eyes narrow at me.

"Yeah," I want to say something clever back; instead, I stare.

"What's your name?"

"Erin."

"I'm Melissa. How old are you?"

I want to be older. I am probably too young to hang out with Melissa. I already know I want to. I think about lying.

"Eleven. Almost twelve."

"I'm twelve," she says. My jaw opens; Melissa already looks like a woman while I, except for two lumps the size of cherries protruding from my chest, still look very firmly a kid. "Can you do a handstand in water?"

I watch as she holds her arms out in front of her and dives in. With the pointed toes of a ballerina, her long, tan legs slice through the surface of the lake in a perfect line. I know I won't be able to do it. When her head breaks through the water, I shake my head.

"Well, I'm going to be in the Olympics someday. As a synchronized swimmer."

I've only ever seen synchronized swimming on TV, and the grace of the limbs under water, the precise movements and timing, it enthralls me. Melissa motions for me to try. I shake my head again.

"It's okay, I'll help you. I'll teach you. You can be my partner." She is not going to take no for an answer, so I take a deep breath and pull through the murky water with my arms. I try to anchor my hands onto the sandy bottom and lift my legs, but I lose my balance and topple over. I come up sputtering. Melissa smiles.

"Everyone starts out like that. Let's do it again. This time, I'll grab your legs and help hold you up." We practice for hours, until our skin is pruned, and the sun goes down, and the pastel pink sunset turns blue around its edges. Still, I can't do a handstand.

The girls in the restaurant take long, slow licks of strawberry ice cream pressed into sugar cones and pad their way back out of the restaurant to their bikes. I watch them pedal away, their wrists that hold the cones rest on the top of the handlebars. I feel a pang in my chest for the instant friendship that childhood provides.

The next morning, I am eager to find Melissa. I've never made such a fast friend before—especially not one so sophisticated. I hop on my bike and comb the campsites and the beach for her but come up empty.

Later that afternoon, I decide to try again and find her standing in front of an enormous travel trailer, the size of a travel bus.

"Melissa!" I call out to her. She waves but stays where she is.

"Is this your place?" I brake just in front of her. I can't tear my gaze from the metallic silver behemoth behind her.

"Uh huh," Melissa said. She is picking at skin on her arm. She does not look up.

"Wow. It's beautiful. Can we go inside?"

Melissa shrugs and opens the door. I step inside gingerly, hoping my sandy feet won't leave a mess. The carpet is a plush off-white colour and my toes sink into the fibres. There is a fireplace with a TV hanging above it, forest green leather couches, and a real fridge and stove. It even has bedrooms and nooks with bunk beds. It is like nothing I've ever seen before. Melissa's face remains blank.

"You must love staying here."

Melissa lets out a laugh. "It's really not that great. Why don't we go to your place?"

Another man wearing a beige canvas hat holds a corner of the newspaper in his left hand and his eyes scan the words. He scoops his meal into his mouth as fast as he can. His haste is peculiar in a beachside restaurant where people typically linger. Again, I pretend to play the game. I imagine a terrible crash where Fred (that's what I've named him) is killed instantly. Even more tragic,

Fred is intolerable and there is nobody but his lonely mother and his boss to attend his funeral. The man looks up from his newspaper as though he feels my gaze on him. His face is worn; his green eyes look sunken from the swollen halfmoons below them, but his face transforms as he smiles politely at me. Immediately, I take back my made-up story about him. I smile back.

We are at Lyle's favourite restaurant to celebrate his promotion to senior project geologist. Lyle raises his glass, and I follow.

"To new accomplishments."

We clink our glasses together. I expect he'll tell me more about the job.

"Your time is coming too."

I nod. Even though I've been there longer than him, I am still an associate.

We kiss madly after tiramisu, and I latch onto him as he guides us through the parking lot under an inky sky. I imagine the promotion to be just one good fortune of many. We drive onto the freeway in his cherry-coloured Miata with the top down. Feeling strangely carefree, I lean my head back and push my arms toward the sky to feel the wind. Lyle takes his eyes off the road to study me. I feel self-conscious; vulnerable.

I swallow the last of my burnt coffee and wipe the toast crumbs from my lips. I shift in my seat, but the skin below my shorts sticks to the burgundy vinyl. The man with the newspaper exits the diner. I watch as he climbs onto a quad. One of the elderly couples stands to leave and the husband guides his wife as they shuffle out, his sturdy hand on her tiny frame. She gazes up at him. They are happy. My hunches about them are right. *Two for two, I* say to myself. *Not bad.* But there is no miserable fate I invent to accompany them.

God, I miss Lyle.

My phone buzzes and I startle.

Why don't you and Lyle come for dinner on Sunday? - sent 8:30 a.m.

It's my mom. I haven't answered her in days. What do I say? *Lyle dumped me for the new intern. I lost my job.* Being let go from the research plant three weeks ago has left me unmoored, directionless.

We are standing in the mint green kitchen of our rental. He is washing dishes so he doesn't have to look at me as he tells me.

"Valerie?!" Valerie is our latest intern at the office. She is at least ten years younger than me. "How? How did this happen?" My voice is high-pitched, pained. Tears blind my vision. I gulp the air, but there is not enough. I shudder and wheeze.

"I don't know what to tell you, Erin." Lyle is calm while I fall apart.

"I thought we were happy," I say. But we both know there have been fissures. Parts of me that don't let Lyle in. I sob. Lyle wipes down a saucer with the dishcloth like any regular Saturday morning. "Why?"

Lyle wrings the cloth out and turns to me.

"She's not as difficult."

I sink down onto the linoleum. For good measure, he plunges the imaginary knife into my gut once more.

I want to smash his face for that.

I throw a five-dollar bill on the table as a tip and peel myself off the chair. It's only a minute's walk to the beach. I hear the rev of boat motors and the squeal of children. The families on the beach stare as I remove my socks and hiking shoes and roll the bottoms of my pant legs up. I'm overdressed for this July weather. I dip my toes at the edge of the water. The girls who bought ice cream cones are in the lake. They shuffle back toward the sand and their beach towels. Their skin is purple and dotted with goosebumps. They are careful not to splash me. I smile as they pass. The area looks much the same: aspen and spruce trees that form a dense canopy on either side of the beach. There are reeds where the lake gets most weedy on one side; grassy banks on the other where boats stop for a short rest. Directly across the water is scrubby and dense forest. I stare down at my pink-cold toes and notice a spotted rock a few inches from my right foot. I bend and scoop the smooth stone into my palm.

We are practicing handstands in the water. Melissa offers to show me some of her synchronized swimming routine. I watch her dance and flip underwater, while humming a tune I don't know when she comes up for air. It doesn't look professional or Olympic-worthy, but who am I to judge? When she finishes, I clap for her. It is better than anything I can do.

As we exit the water, Melissa bends and pulls something out of the murk.

"Hey look, I found quartz!"

I stop, intrigued—I love to find unique looking stones on the gravel pathways and pretend I am discovering something exquisite and rare.

I peer into her hand. It has salt-and-pepper spotted flecks of grey, black, and white. Its distinct appearance is why it caught her eye, but I don't have the heart to tell her it is diorite, a common rock with little quartz.

"I think you should have it," she says. She presses it into my palm and pulls me into a tight hug. I am startled by the force of it.

When I return to our campsite, I add the diorite to the pouch of my favourite stones.

I pocket this new stone in honour of Melissa. I debate peeling off my clothes for a quick dip. I want to capture the blithe feeling of the suspension of time and the weightlessness that swimming might provide. A couple I peg to be in their mid-thirties are wrangling two young children around the ages of two and four. The whole family has manes of terracotta-coloured curls. The four-year-old is singing a Disney song as she digs through the sand around the castle she's built. She could easily be the daughter Lyle and I didn't get to have.

As a child, I loved to dig holes in the coarse sand until my fingernails reached the smooth, cool clay below. Even then I think I knew that I would study the earth; I loved to examine things and dig deeper, discover what I could not yet see. When the girl's hands emerge, her nails are the colour of charcoal. She tries to pick them clean. Her T-shirt is mottled with stains, a layered history of her day. Then she stands and stomps on the sandcastle. The younger one cries at the soft, lumpy ruins. Her father tries to restrain her so that he can strap on her sandals, but the child writhes and wiggles out from his grasp. After several attempts, the father throws the sandals in the beach bag next to them. Happy to be left alone, the little girl nestles into him, and he rubs her back. It's an act of love and it makes me ache for Lyle.

"See? I'm here. I'm dealing with things. I'm taking the steps."
I imagine him beside me, but his likeness glitches like a bad
connection.

*Patio lights emit a half circle glow like oversized fireflies across
Melissa's RV, making their campsite easy to spot. The door swings
open and a man with thick biceps in a white polo steps out and
stops when he sees me. His bleached-tip hair is gelled in place,
frozen on his head. He juggles a large bowl and barbeque tongs.
His legs are tanned and sculpted. He looks nothing like my dad.*

"Is Melissa here?"

*The man resumes his path to the picnic table and sets everything
down.*

*"Who's asking?" He steps towards me. He smells warm like
nutmeg. My belly flips. His eyes dart back and forth like a machine
scanning me. He gets within a foot of me and still doesn't stop. I
lose my balance on my bike seat despite having my right leg act
as a kickstand. No grown man besides my father has ever stood
so close to me.*

*"I'm her friend. Erin," I stammer. His cologne makes me dizzy.
His eyes on me are both thrilling and terrifying. My insides clench
in quick succession. My pulse quickens and the hair on my arms
stand up. I look beyond him to the RV, hoping Melissa comes out.*

*The man smiles. His teeth shine like perfect white pearls. He leans
into me. My mouth goes dry, and my heart thunders in my chest.
I hold my breath. He reaches out with his free hand toward my
face. I squeeze my eyes shut and grip my handlebars, not knowing
what to expect. He tucks a lock of hair around my ear and lets his
fingers linger on the top of my shoulder.*

"Pretty little thing you are." His breath is warm and minty, inviting, but his words make me shrivel into myself. His fingers feel like weapons on me. He slides a finger underneath my spaghetti strap and slides it down until it meets the top of my shirt before snapping the strap and removing his hand. My legs tremble and threaten to collapse. I think about pedalling away as fast as I can, but I remain frozen on the spot.

"Is she here?" My words come out fumbled.

"Melissa!" he calls, finally stepping away from me. He returns to the picnic table. Melissa opens the door. She looks back and forth between the man and me, as if trying to size up the situation.

"Can you play?" I ask her, desperate to leave.

"Yeah, Melissa, can you play?" the man says mocking me.

"Shut up, Dick," Melissa shoots back. My eyes widen. Melissa laughs. "Don't worry. That's really his name. Dick."

I want to laugh but the man has scared me. I just want to go. Melissa hops on her bike and together we ride down an open stretch of road.

"Is that your dad?" I ask.

Melissa shakes her head. "Stepdad. And he's really not a dad to me at all."

I wait for her to say more, but she zips away from me, so I pick up my speed to join her. We pedal as fast as our legs will take us. Our hair flies behind us; the wind makes me feel free. I watch Melissa close her eyes and extend her arms out so that she is riding without any hands. I wish I could do the same, but I am too afraid of crashing and of not seeing what lies ahead. Instead, I keep my hands firmly on my handlebars and steal glances at her—both jealous and in awe of her beauty and her fearlessness.

The sun dips behind a substantial cloud cover that's rolling in and the shadow it creates makes me shiver. I watch the family pack up their belongings into a utility wagon: pails, shovels, inflatable rings, and a mini cooler. My gut lurches. I imagine they leave the lake to take their golden lab for a walk around their brick-faced Colonial perched on ten acres. Inside, they'll play three games of the card game Memory with their children before naptime. The parents will ensure that the kids are settled in their rooms before snuggling on the couch to watch the latest episodes of *Ozark* on Netflix. The husband will caress his wife's face gently before he kisses her, stirring a longing they've had to bury for lack of privacy. The blinds open, the TV still on, the combination of the daring characters on the show and the rare opportunity for time alone will spur him to press for more. They'll make love gently on the couch while the action of the show erupts through the speakers and rays of afternoon sunlight spill across their bodies. I want to play the game and imagine that it ends differently because it's easier to imagine tragedy. My ability to imagine this strange couple's amazing life together is stabbing and cruel, but I can't invent a different storyline for them. I am older than they are, but I have nothing to show for my life. Not even a job.

I bike over to Melissa's hoping to spend my last few hours of vacation with her. Again, her stepdad is outside. He does not look like someone camping in his shiny golf shirt and pleated shorts.

"Erin!" He greets me with enthusiasm. "Why don't you have a seat? Melissa just went to get us some buns from the store."

"It's okay. I'll go find her."

"She's probably just around the corner. Best to wait for her here." He motions to the lawn chair beside him. I don't want to stay, but I hear my mother's instruction to always be polite to people play in my mind, and I don't want to be rude, so I hop off my bike and take

I rub my eyes. My skin prickles. I want to peel it off my bones.
Recall steals my breath.

"We'll get you cleaned up. Please, come in."

My body screams at me to get on my bike and leave, but I want to do as I'm told. Plus, I've got blood dripping everywhere and it's embarrassing. I follow, reluctant.

Dick passes me a damp cloth he's warmed with hot water. It smells like floral laundry detergent. I wipe my hands and then pinch my nose with it. I am careful to stand on the linoleum so that I don't get blood on their nice carpet. Dick steps close to me.

"Let me have a look," he says. He presses himself against me. I hold my breath. He takes my hand and pulls the washcloth back. "It looks much better now."

His voice is low, raspy.

"I better go," I say. He presses into me harder and my back digs into the countertop. I want to cry out, but I stand stock-still. He envelops me so that there is no exit. His hand reaches between my legs, and he rubs me roughly. I squeeze my eyes closed again and whimper. Then, I hear the zipper of his shorts.

"No, please…" But he does not listen. And Melissa does not come right back.

Rage flows under the surface of me like burning magma. For twenty years, it has bubbled and festered and eroded me from the inside out. If you were to dig through to my core, I burn hotter than the sun. A representation of the centre of the earth. How could a geologist not understand that analogy?

The day he carries boxes out of our house I decide to speed up the process. I pick up odds and ends that cannot be boxed like the coat rack and fling it onto the lawn.

"What are you doing?!" Lyle races back into the house. He reaches for me, but I drag his golf clubs past him and hurl them outside. They clatter upon hitting the pavement and scatter like a game of Pick-Up Sticks. "Are you serious, Erin?"

I stand with my arms crossed. I don't care how I'm acting.

"There are people who can help you," Lyle says. "You don't have to be alone in this." Then he leaves me.

One of the young girls in the bathing suits startles me. She has come back to look for something she's lost. My face is wet from crying, and I work to dry my face so that I don't scare the poor girl. I notice her colt-like legs, how she bends and walks and carries herself with a self-assurance I have never known. She moves the sand underfoot with pointed toes, as though whatever she has lost might be unearthed. She jumps, suddenly aware that I am there too.

I picture Melissa and how she surprised me in the water, her handstands, and the two of us on our bikes sailing down the open road. I imagine her hair blowing behind her, her eyes squeezed shut and her arms out. How carefree and daring I thought her to be.

Lyle's image appears next to me. "Are we playing the game or what?" He's wiry and lean in his swim shorts and I want to nestle into him. I nod. Anything to keep him around.

I try to invent a tragic fate for this young girl, who reminds me so much of Melissa, but nothing comes. Instead, I want to hug her. Sometimes you just know when a person has been through enough. The game isn't fun anymore.

Misfortune

That morning, just before eight, Oscar unlocked the door of Mega-Save Hardware, turned on the lights, and washed the grime off the windows from the dust storm that had blown through the night before. He swept the sidewalk out front, pushed the tangled tumbleweeds onto the asphalt of the road with the head of his broom. Finally, he flipped the plastic sign on the door from "closed" to "open."

Oscar studied the building. He noted the new chunks of stucco that were missing from the building's façade. He swept his index finger across the wooden sill of the front window. The wood crumbled in his hands. The inside was no less a worry. The ceiling bowed down toward the brittle, chipped linoleum at the rear of the store. Even the floors had a distinct slant that made customers compensate when moving from aisles one through four.

Oscar, a man with more shine than hair on his head and a back that demanded a slow gait, had been contemplating closing the store after thirty-four years. There were fewer customers each year, especially since they'd built that big box development in the small city thirty minutes away. At one time he'd been passionate about his work, but his attempts at keeping the store alive now were half-hearted at best.

Oscar shuffled some of the merchandise around, hoping to fill in some of the gaps on his shelving. He would not replace the stock. There was a time he'd had a staff of twelve. It had been a few years since he'd needed an employee to help with the store. He had Payton Lewis, his neighbour's daughter and a newly-minted accountant, taking care of the books. Otherwise, he was it.

When the classic jangle of the bell above the store's entrance sounded, Oscar straightened and smoothed the wiry silver behind his ears, should any of the hair be wayward. If his store was falling apart, he wanted to, at the very least, present himself as a man who was well put-together.

Life had not prepared Oscar for the woman who entered his store. Short and waif-like, her glossy bob glistened like silky caramel under the store's fluorescent lights. Oscar was sure he had not seen her before. He watched her floral multi-coloured dress swirl around her ankles as she walked. She spotted him and approached as though they were long lost friends meeting again.

"Hello! Oscar, is it?" She reached for his hands and squeezed them. Her cool fingers were polished in red. Oscar looked down and surprised himself by noticing that she wasn't wearing any rings. He couldn't recall ever having noticed that about someone before.

"Yes, I'm Oscar," he stammered. He waited to see what she'd say next. Her green eyes were rimmed with black eyeliner. She wore heavy mascara and a matching scarlet on her lips. The lipstick was what betrayed her otherwise youthful appearance. It settled into the cracks of her lips and bled into the tiny wrinkles around her mouth. It seemed like a lot of fanfare for everyday shopping in their small town and Oscar was taken by her glamour.

"Hello! I'm Nancy. New to town." She continued squeezing his hands. Oscar felt himself flush at the intimacy of it. "I heard you might be looking for an employee?"

Oscar's eyes narrowed. "Who said that?" He couldn't imagine anyone recommending the Mega-Save as a place to work. Everyone knew the store was failing. How would he pay her when the store had been hemorrhaging money for months?

"It turns out, I have lots of experience running a store. I think I'm just what this place needs," she cooed. She leaned into him. "Nancy Perlinger, dear." He could smell the vanilla tones of her perfume. He stared at her blood-red lips and pictured kissing her, even though he hadn't kissed a woman in thirty years. His gut stirred. Oscar blinked as though he were dreaming, this beautiful woman waltzing into his store, practically throwing herself into him and wanting to work. He cleared his throat again, unsure if his words would be coherent.

"I could use someone here," he found himself saying. "If you are looking for work."

"I can get started right now, if you'll let me." She dropped his hands and sashayed behind the cash register. She placed her hands on the counter and looked around. "The first thing we should do is fix that window display. Since it's camping season, you should have those things front and centre."

She gathered items from the shelves, even unboxing some of them. Oscar scratched his head and watched, speechless. He thought about stopping her, but he was too curious about what she'd do next. An hour later, she had set up a makeshift campsite just beyond the front entry. She'd placed some of the plastic garden gnomes around the propane fire pit as if they were having a campfire. She dragged the dusty plastic fiscus tree to the rear of the display and strung the second last box of patio lights atop it, even plugging them in. A warm glow transformed the stark space.

Oscar wasn't sure if all this was necessary. After all, he needed customers to enter the store to see the changes. Nancy seemed to know just what to do. She pulled out a rickety sandwich board from the back and asked Oscar for a marker. He rummaged through the drawer of the desk where the cash register was and found one. He watched as Nancy's long and lilting scrawl announced a sale of thirty percent off camping gear for the weekend. Oscar had never held many sales in the store, instead he'd always tried to price the items affordably. Rather than stop her, he watched as she set the sandwich board on the sidewalk. To his surprise, they had four customers before noon who made purchases.

The next morning, Nancy blew into the store. This time, she wore an emerald pantsuit and matching heels. Large green hoops hung from her ears. She'd even matched her eyeshadow to her outfit. On someone else, it might be too much, but Oscar was taken by her attention to detail. Nancy came toward him with the same swift energy as the day before. He felt a palpitation in his chest. She grabbed his hand and pulled him to the front windows. She'd added potted red geraniums the same colour as her lipstick to the front of the building and at the base of the sandwich board. He watched Nancy's eyes dance. His lips curled up in a genuine smile that reached all the way to his eyes.

More townspeople stopped in, some just to chat with Oscar, curious about the changes they'd noticed outside. Oscar was thrilled with the activity. There was a lightness to him that he hadn't felt in a long time. He found himself humming, arranging stock with better care. He was already imagining what the two of them could do. There was winter stock to be ordered. He knew Nancy would create something even bigger for Christmas if he planned the order right. Nancy appeared with a bottle of cleaning spray and a dirty rag.

"The shelves are all done now. Things are looking great."

Oscar nodded. "I don't know how to thank you for all of your hard work," he said.

Oscar was about to ask more about her: where she was from, her work history, why she'd chosen their small town to move to—but they were interrupted by his neighbour, Abe Lewis.

"Oscar, did you hear about Lou Anderson?"

Lou used to own the gas station before health problems had forced him to sell. He became a drinker and gained another fifty pounds. Oscar knew the news couldn't be good.

"He's got stomach cancer. Stage four, I think. Heard they're scared they are going to lose the farm now too."

Oscar shook his head. Lou was a good guy. A hard worker. Life had been rough on him and his wife Debbie throughout the years. He pictured the Anderson homestead and a realty sign at the edge of their gravel driveway. The thought made his breakfast swim in his belly. Nancy cocked her head at the two men and stepped toward them. She reached out her hand to shake Abe's.

"Oh, yes, sorry. Abe, this is Nancy." Oscar pointed to Abe. "He's my neighbour. Nancy, here, is my new employee."

Abe's eyes scanned Nancy first and shifted around the store. "Business must be good then." He craned his neck further to get a better look at the store. Although he didn't say anything, Oscar could feel Abe's disbelief. He had a feeling that Abe knew Oscar's numbers since his daughter was the one who did his accounting for him. Abe turned back to the front door. His eyes rested on the camping display, and he smiled. They bid each other goodbye, and Nancy reached for Oscar's hands again.

"I know just what to do!"

Oscar grew warm. Her words electrified him. With Nancy, it seemed anything was possible.

"We'll start a collection for him. Or a GoFundMe."

"For Lou?" Oscar asked. "What's a GoFundMe?"

"It's a website. It collects donations on behalf of someone."

Oscar raised his eyebrows. Donations could really help the Andersons.

"A person writes the details of the cause, and the money appears directly into the account after someone has donated electronically. And we'll set out a collection box at the counter and ask customers for donations."

"I don't know anything about computers," Oscar admitted. The new technologies scared him. It had been a big deal to bring in the debit machine a decade ago and truth be told, he still preferred cash.

"I can take care of it all. I'll have it set up and ready for donations before the hour is through." Nancy took out her cell phone.

"What are their names again?" Nancy asked.

"Lou and Debbie Anderson. Debbie with an 'ie.'" Oscar's eyes widened as her thumbs typed furiously. Oscar could picture himself trying to do the same thing—his index finger circling around the characters until he found the letter he needed, always pressing one letter at a time.

In just minutes, the GoFundMe was ready. Then Nancy disappeared into the back and returned with a box wrapped in Kraft paper. She cut a slit into the top for the money to be dropped into. She wrote on the side of the box with the marker.

For the next few weeks, every time a customer approached the till, Nancy and Oscar showed them the box. Each customer donated. Oscar watched Nancy interact with them, her delicate, sun-spotted hand often placed on their shoulder or on top of their hand if it were close enough to her. Her warmth and gentle touch seemed to transfix every single person who encountered her. The fact that she'd go through the trouble to create a fundraiser for a man she didn't even know made tears spring to his eyes.

Oscar fell into bed each night, his feet and back good and sore. He felt the satisfaction of a hard day's work. He also found himself fantasizing about Nancy and the image of her chatting with the customers, her charismatic smile charming everyone around her. She always left for the night before he did. He tried to imagine where she lived and what she was wearing to bed at night. He pictured her long, slender fingers and those red nails travelling down his naked body, and he shivered. He hadn't been with anyone in decades, knew nothing of the modern dating world and how it all worked.

He started to hear from other customers how generous Nancy was to them.

"She gave me a box of electrical outlet covers for free. Threw them in when she saw how my little Oliver was getting into everything," a young mom with a toddler in tow said.

"That Nancy. She gave me some ant killer to try, said I could try it for free, and would you believe, it worked like a charm?"

For a moment, Oscar cringed at hearing things being given without being charged, but he saw the customer return and buy two bottles of ant killer. Maybe he'd been using the wrong sales tactics his whole life.

At the end of the month, Oscar tripled his order for the store. With the increased traffic, he didn't want to risk losing customers due to low stock. He could scarcely believe that at the beginning of August, he'd contemplated not ordering anything at all. He wondered if the store had ever been as bustling as it was now or if his sales had ever been this good.

At the end of a particularly profitable rainy day, Oscar flipped the sign to closed. His chest felt full. His shoulders were relaxed, limbs loose. Excited, he reached for Nancy and pulled her close to him. He could feel her breasts against his chest, the warmth of her breath against his neck. She laughed, but it was a high-pitched sound that wobbled with uncertainty. At once, Oscar drew back, embarrassed at what had come over him. How could he hug her without her permission? How forward and uncouth it felt to do something so out of character for him. He hoped he hadn't scared her away.

"I'm so sorry," Oscar said, his eyes closed. "I didn't mean to overstep." He wanted to tell her what a difference she'd made in the store, in him, and how grateful he was for her, but no words would come. She would not meet his eyes. He watched as she gathered her purse and the umbrella she'd brought with her and left the store quickly.

The next day, she didn't come in. There was no phone call, no note left on the door for him. He realized then that he didn't even have her number. She'd never missed a day since she'd started. Oscar blamed himself for her absence, sure that his hug had crossed boundaries and damaged their relationship somehow. He watched the door all day, but it was never her stepping through the entrance.

"Where's Nancy?" customers asked.

"Not in today," Oscar said. He tried to be as jovial as she'd been, but he knew he lacked the magnetism Nancy had. She was the missing ingredient to the store's success.

At three in the afternoon, the bell sounded, and Lou and Debbie Anderson appeared in view. Lou was in a wheelchair and Debbie fumbled to keep the door open while pushing the wheelchair through. Oscar rushed over, helping to bring the chair fully inside the store. He was startled by Lou's appearance, his gaunt face, his once husky frame and ample girth reduced to a spindle wrapped tightly in an afghan. White whisps of hair stood up in patches on his head. Debbie had large rings around her eyes that spoke of sleepless nights and the kind of worry and grief that changed a person.

"We wanted to come in and say thank you in person …" Debbie said. Her eyes filled with tears and she couldn't continue.

"It means a lot," Lou said, his voice feeble. He reached out his hand, the skin over his bones so thin it looked like it could tear at the slightest touch. Oscar felt his throat tighten and shook Lou's hand.

"Anything to help. Anything at all."

"We heard the account was almost at $10,000 already," Debbie said. "That money will help us get by, especially since I had to leave work."

Oscar nodded. He wished he could do even more. He thought about giving them whatever was in the donation box so that they could see that he'd been trying to collect for them in multiple ways. He turned to the register but noticed for the first time that day that the box wasn't there. They hadn't moved it since Nancy first put it out. He looked again to make sure his eyes weren't playing tricks on him. It was not there.

"Anything I can get for you from here? Whatever you need. Take it. It's yours." Oscar gestured to the aisles. His heart quickened. Where was the box? Was it in the back room? His stomach started to swim. He didn't want the Andersons to detect his newfound concern.

"We're just fine but thank you." Debbie said. "That money will be a real blessing. Already we've fallen behind on the mortgage. Knowing that money is there for us—it's a real godsend." She choked back a sob and tucked the blanket tighter around her husband's frame. Oscar felt his nose tickle and his eyes fill with tears. He stared at Lou's grey house slippers, then Debbie spun the chair back toward the door.

"I'll make sure you get some of that money right away then," Oscar called after them. "No need for all this worrying when so many folks want to help out. Money's the last thing to be worrying about."

Debbie and Lou exited the store. Oscar watched from the front window as Debbie pushed Lou down the sidewalk. He watched Debbie stop and wipe her eyes. He felt both heavy and light inside, knowing that good could come from misfortune. He walked back to the till but could not see the donation box. He walked to the back room in case it had been stored for safekeeping. It was not there.

Oscar tried to keep his mind off the missing box. He set to watering the geraniums outside, wiping down the shelves that hadn't yet acquired any dust, and imagined the revamp of the store with all the inventory that was on its way.

He hoped he'd hear from Nancy. He replayed his spirited hug over in his mind, desperate to see her and make things right between them again. He'd do whatever it took because he realized in that moment that he was in love with her. She'd waltzed into the store and into his life and upended everything in the most unexpected way, and he'd never been happier.

Three days later, the RCMP pulled up alongside the store. Oscar's lips trembled. Had something terrible happened to Nancy? He smoothed his hair down and fidgeted with the dusting cloth in his hands. The two officers approached the cash register, their boots making loud thumps against the floor.

"How can I help you, officers?" He didn't recognize either of them, but constables were being transferred around the province all the time. Oscar also led a quiet life, one that didn't interact with the police all that much.

"We're looking for someone," one of them said. He held out a photo. The woman's hair was dyed blonde with grey roots. She wore little make-up and looked tired and washed out. But there was no mistaking that the woman in the photo was Nancy. Without the bob, the eye make-up, and the lipstick. "We understand that she may have been working here."

"Nancy. Nancy Perlinger. Is she okay?" Oscar let his mind imagine a car crash or an accidental drowning. Something tragic. How then could he make things right between them? He'd never forgive himself.

"I'm afraid this isn't Nancy. This is Julie Parsons. Goes by a number of different aliases, though."

Oscar swallowed. "Aliases? What do you mean?"

"She's wanted across the country for fraud. Likes to frequent sleepy little towns and bilk them for all she can."

Oscar let the words sink in. He pictured the donation box. He thought of the GoFundMe. His mouth went dry.

"Can you tell us where she might be?" The officer said. "Do you have any contact information for her?"

Oscar felt himself tremble. He could feel a pulsating in his temples. He had the sensation of prickles down his spine.

"You okay, sir?" One of the constables studied him.

Oscar was sure he'd turned grey. He could barely stay upright.

"I don't. I never got any. I paid her at the end of each week. She just showed up every day." Oscar felt stupid. "It's not how I'd normally do business, but I was thinking of closing and then she came and…" Oscar began to sob. "She changed everything around in such a short time. I thought she'd been a miracle."

The officers nodded. One of them wrote in a notebook while Oscar spoke.

"There's one more thing," Oscar said. "A donation. For the Andersons. A box of money and a GoFundMe page."

The constable who was writing locked eyes with him. "Of course, there was." He sighed and shook his head.

"So, you're saying you think she's taken the money?" Oscar said. "Are you sure we're talking about the same person? She doesn't look like this one," he said, pointing to the woman in the photo. "She has brown hair, it's shiny and cut straight like this," he motioned with his hands. Even as he argued it, Oscar knew it to be true.

"She's been known to alter her appearance. It's all part of her act."

Oscar felt unsteady on his feet. He reached for a chair nearby and slid it beside the check-out so that he could sit down.

The officers left him a card and remarked at what a great store he had, how they'd never been in it before but would be back. Oscar stayed in the chair, staring at the wall. He wished for Nancy to come through the door so that he could convince himself it wasn't true. He wished for the donation box and the funds from the donation page so that he could give it to the Andersons. He wished he'd shut the store down when he'd had the chance—before Nancy had walked in and changed everything. Regret was a bitter pill. Even worse was the feeling of being robbed. He thought of Lou in his wheelchair, his tear-stained face and gratitude for the money that would allow them to keep their house. Only now, the money was likely long gone.

Oscar looked at the camping display, at the silly gnomes with their plastic smiles as though they were mocking him for his ignorance. He hung on to the fiscus tree for stability and kicked a gnome across the room, its face caving in. He kicked at the others, each of them flying through the store and crashing into shelves. He picked up the firepit and spun it like an oversized frisbee, the rocks soaring like fireworks as they catapulted off the products.

He flung the lantern, watched it break into thousands of pieces. He wrested the makeshift walls around the display and as they crumbled toward the ground, he stomped on them. He tore apart every single part of Nancy's work until it looked like his store had been ransacked. He was out of breath, wheezing. His shirt mopped up his sweat and left wide wet circles on him. His wiry hair sprung away from his ears and straight up, much like a mad scientist. He destroyed it all, sat in one of the camp chairs to catch his breath, and put his head in his hands.

Then the bell jangled. A young man in a blue ball cap and coveralls stood at the entrance, stunned. He looked at the mess and at Oscar.

"Can I help you?" Oscar said, still breathing hard.

"A shipment, sir. Just wondering where you'd like it."

Oscar took in the absurdity of it all—the stock he wished he hadn't ordered, the missing money for the Andersons, the damage he'd inflicted in his own store. There was only one thing he could do to make it right again.

"Well, let's get it unloaded then." Oscar said. "I've got a lot to sell."

The young man shifted uncomfortably. He clearly didn't know what to make of the scene.

"Got lots of stuff for you then, sir."

"Ten thousand dollars' worth, I hope." Oscar said.

He had a store to clean and to stock. Sales to be instituted. Winter gear and a Christmas display to create. A farm to save. Money to raise. Good could always come out of misfortune.

Counting Through It

Dina stacked the dirty plates and set them on the granite counter. The dishwasher hummed with a mouthful of lunch dishes. Now, four place settings and a mismatch of glassware waited for their turn. James would be home from work soon. Or so he said. Day often bled into the night before she'd hear the rumble of the garage door opening, signaling his arrival. There were meetings, drinks, rounds of golf, overtime. Circumstances that James insisted were part and parcel of making partner one day.

That morning, Dina sat nursing the baby on their bed and observed James buttoning his cufflinks in front of the mirror. He posed, regal in a crisp, grey Italian suit worth more than what she'd spent on her own wardrobe since she'd given birth to their first baby. He spun from his hip to get a side view of himself and smoothed the ivory silk shirt that skimmed his taut abdomen. Once upon a time, his physique and trendy fashion sense had impressed her and made her feel fortunate. They'd made a handsome pair. Now, her own belly spilled from the elastic waistband of her pants and spread like bread dough around her. Her head throbbed with intense envy at his ability to leave the house so polished.

James, satisfied with his attire, moved to his hair. She pictured spilling coffee on him or the baby vomiting on his shoulder. Something to keep him in the trenches with her. He whistled as he finished combing his hair with his fingers and checked himself one last time before he stepped away from the mirror, kissed her on the forehead, and exited their bedroom. Dina peered down at her now stretched, threadbare grade-twelve gym T-shirt that clung to her engorged breasts. She couldn't remember the last time she'd worn another type of outfit or gone shopping in a bricks-and-mortar store instead of clicking on discount stretch pants online.

Now, as night descended, Dina watched the crisp amber leaves skip along the pavement under the streetlight. She closed the blinds in the living room. She tossed the menagerie of toys that littered the floor into wicker baskets. She folded the last of the laundered towels from their trip to the swimming pool and carried the basket of laundry up the stairs. As if on cue, she heard the deep, barking coughs of two of her three children. Dina flinched at the sound. Surely, there couldn't be another virus in circulation. They'd just made it through strep throat a couple of weeks earlier. She set the basket down and peered into the dark bedrooms, but the children were still in their beds. Dina blew her overgrown bangs from her eyes and decided she'd turn on the TV downstairs and fold another basket of clothes.

She thought she'd wanted this—leaving her caseworker position to stay home and raise the kids. Her own mother had stayed home with her until she started school. Initially, Dina had certified as a fitness instructor and taught a spin class a few nights a week. She'd enjoyed it. It had been enough of a balance. By the time they'd had two children, James worked longer hours and she could no longer justify the cost of childcare while she was teaching at the gym. She'd been home full-time ever since. She'd also quit working out altogether. She couldn't remember the last time she'd carved out time for exercise. Her muscles had atrophied, and she'd morphed into a soft, plumper version of herself. The days were beginning to blur into an endless monotony of trying to please cranky kids and keep their four walls together.

On her way to the TV, Dina glimpsed the tired, yellow Dianthuses that hung limp from the vase on the middle of the dining table. The murky water smelled sharp, and the petals had shrivelled. Dina had let them fester in the water too long. She spotted the kids' plastic plates sitting there from bedtime snack. She'd carefully quartered the grapes. She'd cut cheese slices into shapes using cookie cutters, with the requisite thinness that the children insisted upon. Most had bites taken out of them but were largely uneaten and would likely be wasted. Although Dina often ate the leftovers on their plates, she wasn't hungry. She hadn't been eating well for days now. She waved at the fruit flies that circled the food bits. With the cool fall weather and the harvest of their small garden, the tiny bugs had taken residence in her dining room. She moved the plates onto the waiting stack of dishes in the kitchen.

"Mommy?"

Dina was startled by the sound of her son's voice. Her first instinct was to yell. How hard was it to go to bed and stay in bed?

She set the plates down and shut her eyes. She took a deep breath before answering.

"Yes? What is it?" Austin, as the oldest, was the one child she could usually count on to help her or to listen. "You're supposed to be in bed."

"I know, Mommy, but you need to come upstairs. Sydney's sick."

"Again? I didn't hear anything…" Dina looked up at the video monitor that rested on the kitchen island. There, she could see her two-year-old curled up in a ball on the floor. Sydney liked to press the buttons on the monitor, and she'd muted it without Dina noticing. She flicked on the sound. Another sharp bark of a cough and a whine. Dina's whole body tensed.

Austin followed her up the stairs. Before reaching Sydney's room, Dina peeked into the master bedroom. Her eyes searched for the baby's figure in the maple crib stationed across from her own bed. She watched for any movement, but three-month-old Sarah was still. Dina said a silent prayer of thanks to the darkened room. At least one of her children was sleeping.

Dina tiptoed past. The light from the hallway cast a path of golden light on the carpet that led to Sydney and her head of dark curls. Sydney's newly acquired "big girl" bed that she'd been so excited to sleep in was still dressed in pale pink cotton, the edges crisp and tight. Dina imagined her toddler crawling out of the top of the bed as gingerly as she could, so as not to ruffle the pretty covers.

"Mommy's just going to scoop you up," Dina whispered, reaching down for her. Sydney's bangs stuck to her forehead. Dina touched her wrist to the girl's slick skin. It burned to the touch. When Dina put her arms under her child, Sydney flopped into her, listless. How could she be sick again? Hadn't the antibiotics done their job?

Dina wheezed after she got downstairs with her. Her own exhaustion made her dizzy and disoriented. She hadn't slept a full night in months and could feel a scratchiness in her throat. She set Sydney on the living room sectional and walked to the bathroom to get the thermometer. Before she could pull it from the medicine cabinet, she heard the first retch. Dina closed her eyes and took a deep breath. Surely, this was not happening.

"Mooommmyyyy!" Austin called. She thought she'd sent him back to bed, but he was sitting at the base of the staircase, monitoring his sister.

"I know. Mommy can take care of this. Back up to bed."

Austin's chestnut hair, still damp from his evening bath, was mussed from tossing in his bed. He bit his lip and turned back up the stairs.

The contents of Sydney's stomach had splattered across the couch and the area rug in a spectacular burst. Dina's own gut felt twisted and pressured as if vice grips had taken residence and wrung her insides out. Sydney had curled back up into herself, but she'd rolled right through the mess. Dina cupped her mouth. She could feel tears building at the corners of her eyes. She looped her arms under her daughter's tiny frame and carried her back to the bathroom. She peeled off Sydney's nightgown, balled it up and threw it into the hallway. She realized her own shirt was soiled too. She pulled it off and continued in just her nursing bra and pants. She set her little one in the bathtub and tested the water before letting the shower head rain down. Sydney whimpered.

"I know, sweetie. Mommy's just trying to get you cleaned up. I'll be quick." Dina poured a generous amount of body wash into her palm and worked quickly to rub Sydney's hair and body down. She didn't want to risk making her fever worse by having the water too hot or by having Sydney shiver. After a thorough rinse, Dina shut the tap off and grabbed a towel from the hook. She enveloped her daughter in the towel and then into her arms, grateful for the faint scent of gardenias that now filled the room.

Dina's legs shook as she carried Sydney upstairs. Her foot fumbled on the second last step and Dina pitched forward, almost face-planting on the landing. She used an arm on the handrail to pull herself vertical again, but her back wrenched from the correction and the weight of carrying Sydney. Dina stood at the top of the stairs, a steady throb in her back, her breath a shrill whistle. When she'd reoriented herself, she walked by her bedroom and willed her baby girl to stay asleep. This time, she could see Sarah fidgeting in her crib.

She looked at the alarm clock on Sydney's end table. 9:07 p.m. James should have been home by now. She pulled the first nightgown she could find from the dresser and quickly slipped it over her daughter's head. She set her back into her bed and then placed the thermometer in Sydney's ear and waited for the beep. 102.5.

"Is she okay?" It was Austin again, peeking his head through the doorway.

"Yes, she'll be fine. I'm just going to give her some medicine," Dina said. "Back to bed. You need to go to sleep now." There was an edge to her voice. Austin turned back to his room.

They kept the medication in their ensuite bathroom to keep it further from the kids' curious hands. Dina tiptoed through her bedroom, her eyes on Sarah's tossing figure. She flicked on the light, bristled from the harshness of it and let her eyes adjust. She opened the childproof lock of the cabinet as quietly as she could and fished out the children's liquid Tylenol.

Dina went downstairs to the utensil drawer to find the little syringe they used to dispense medication. She knew Sydney preferred the little cup that came in the box, but she hoped her daughter wouldn't notice. Using the syringe would allow Dina to squirt the medicine in the side of Sydney's mouth without completely waking her. The loud clanks of metal as she searched for the syringe set her nerves further on edge.

She spotted the syringe and grabbed it. She had to grip the handrail as she climbed back up the stairs. Sweat prickled her temples and armpits. A wave of dizziness set her off balance and her hand flew to her forehead. Was she developing a fever too?

Dina pre-measured the medicine into the syringe and lined it up with Sydney's lips.

"Here's some medicine to make you feel better, Sydney," Dina whispered. She pressed the edge of the syringe and was grateful that Sydney started sucking on the medicine as it entered her mouth. When the last of it was dispensed, she pressed her lips to her daughter's cheek, then turned to leave. Just as she crossed the threshold of Sydney's room, there was a cry.

Dina let out her breath. Sarah. She was awake. Dina plodded to the crib and replaced Sarah's soother. With any luck, she'd fall right back asleep. Sarah's eyes were still closed, and she sucked vigorously for about thirty seconds before spitting it out. She let out a wail.

"Shhh!" Dina said, hoping to soothe her and limit the noise so that the other two children wouldn't wake. Sarah's eyes flew open, and she cried harder.

Dina picked Sarah up. The baby could smell Dina's milk-stained bra and immediately, she tried to suckle through the fabric. When Dina tried rocking the baby instead, she wailed back. She had just fed her before she'd put her down, but Sarah was demanding to be fed again. Dina gave in, took root in the rocking chair in the corner of her and James' room and unhooked her bra.

Sarah suckled madly. Dina stroked the dimples that punctuated her daughter's tiny hand. This act of nourishing a human that she'd grown within her womb—their hearts beating and blood pumping through them at the same time in the same vessel—and how her body had what it needed to provide and when, was a miracle of the human body. The two of them sat in the dark to the sound of Sarah's gulping and swallowing. Dina could feel the steady rhythm of Sarah's breathing against her. She found herself counting to it. *One, two, three…* this rhythm grounded her to the moment of her baby content in her arms.

Dina wiped her brow and felt a bead of sweat trickling under her breasts and onto her abdomen from the warmth of Sarah's body. Her head throbbed along with her back now. The darkness of the room made her eyelids droop, but she did not want to fall asleep in the chair and risk dropping the baby. Her eyes grew heavy. She pinched at her forearm to keep from dozing. When Sarah's suckling slowed, Dina held her upright to burp her. She cupped Sarah's chin in her hand and patted her back gently, but nothing came. She changed positions and placed her over her shoulder, but there was no burp there either. Sarah grew fussy with Dina's movements or from discomfort, Dina couldn't tell, so Dina tried to rock her back to sleep. Sarah's fussing turned into a full-blown cry.

"*What,* baby?!" Dina pleaded. Sarah's cry intensified and Dina set her down on the bed. She looked for anything that might be poking the baby but could find nothing. She checked her diaper, but it was only lightly soiled with pee. She changed her anyway and Sarah screamed through the whole thing.

"Mommy?" It was Austin again. "Is Sarah okay?"

Dina blinked. "She is *fine*. Go to bed!"

Austin ran back to his room at the tone of his mother's voice. Dina immediately regretted her words. He was just looking out for his sisters. She'd go back and talk to him. Apologize and kiss him goodnight when Sarah settled again.

She thought back to when Austin was a baby. How lucky they were with how easy he was to take care of as first-time parents. He'd slept through the night by six weeks old. When he woke, he'd have his chubby feet in his hands, smiling, waiting patiently for Dina to collect him. She'd adored sitting in the glider with him for long stretches. Life had moved slower then, and she'd had time to soak up the gifts of motherhood. The time felt like she'd always gained far more than what it had taken from her.

Dina bounced Sarah on her thighs, made laps around the room with her laid across her arm, and placed her on the bed and made bicycle movements with her legs in case she had a stomachache. Any position she tried seemed to have no effect on her daughter's screaming. She felt for a temperature but realized how futile that was without the thermometer. Sarah had made herself flushed and sweaty with her displeasure.

She centered Sarah on her bed and rushed into Sydney's room, remembering that she'd taken Sydney's temperature from her bed. She placed the thermometer in Sarah's ear, but her temperature was normal. Dina was thankful.

She grabbed a receiving blanket and held Sarah to her shoulder to go back down to the main floor. There, they could pace until James returned home and hopefully Sarah wouldn't wake the other two. Just as they reached the bottom of the stairs, the smell of Sydney's vomit permeated the air. She'd forgotten about the mess.

Dina winced and veered to the kitchen. Sarah continued to cry. Dina unsnapped the baby's sleeper to cool her off. Their sweaty skins stuck to one another as Dina circled the kitchen island over and over. She had to pee but tried not to think about it.

Dina's phone lit up from the kitchen counter. She dove for it, eager for any kind of distraction from the crying. She hoped it was James, saying he was on his way home.

Just having a drink with Lonny. Be home soon. -sent 10:42 p.m.

Of course, he was. Drinks with the founder of the firm were never turned down. Getting in with Lonny meant that you might be somebody there someday. Dina chucked the phone down and it clattered onto the granite counter. She debated telling him she needed him to come home right now but knew he wouldn't.

Five years ago, at James' presentation to the bar, she'd clapped louder than anyone in the room when his name was announced. They'd both imagined how their lives might change after law school and then the year of articling. It had been a long haul. Slater and Sommers Law Firm hiring him had felt like the real start of their lives together. Just weeks later, they'd found this house and closed on it quickly. On their possession day, James had placed sticky notes on the other bedroom doors besides the master that read, "Future Baby Johnson" and Dina's belly had fluttered as if it were that easy to label something and make it so.

Dina would show James how angry she was when he got home. She imagined he'd tell her later, "What was I supposed to do? Leave my boss sitting there all alone?"

"You'd tell him there was a family emergency."

"It wasn't an emergency, Dina," he'd say. But it felt like one. Even though she could see nothing physically wrong with Sarah, she could not get her to stop crying. Tears darted out from the edges of her eyes. Sarah's fists were balled up and her body was rigid. Dina could feel her breasts working overtime, continuous taps leaking through her bra at her baby's cries. She tried letting her suckle again, but Sarah batted at her breasts with her tiny fists.

Finally, Dina placed her in the motorized baby swing and turned it on. Sarah twisted in the seat, her fists swinging at the air. Dina ran to the bathroom to finally pee and found the distance from the crying a relief of its own. She washed her hands and caught a glimpse of herself in the mirror. Dark circles made her eyes look hollow. Her hair was greasy, and half pulled from its ponytail. Her bra was yellowed and soaked. The mixture of sweat and milk dribbled down her torso and wet the elastic band of her pants. She was surprised to see that she'd been crying. Her nipples felt raw as if they'd been shredded through a cheese grater. She splashed cold water on her face, kicked Sydney's vomit-covered nightgown further down the hall, and returned to Sarah's screams.

Leaving her in the swing had angered the baby even more. Her face took on a purple tinge that alarmed Dina. She held the baby close and then placed her onto the island to examine her again. Sarah flailed at the cold granite on her sweaty skin. Dina couldn't find anything wrong. She ran her fingers across Sarah's gums to check for any teeth that might be trying to find their way through, but there was nothing out of the ordinary.

Dina looked across at her phone, which was upside down next to the toaster. She stared at it for a moment before retrieving it to type James a message.

You need to come home. Kids are sick. 11:04 p.m.

Would he even take a moment from his conversation with Lonny to check his phone? Or would that jeopardize his career? Dina's jaw clamped. She knew her own exhaustion was a factor in her iciness to James. Aside from nursing, he'd been an equal participant tending to their children at night. He'd shuffle through the house as bleary-eyed as she was, fulfilling needs—a sippy cup, a fallen stuffed animal, nightmares about monsters or a sore throat. But for the past couple of months, she consistently found herself staring at their bedroom ceiling while James and the rest of the family slumbered peacefully around her. She knew how even a bit more sleep could make all the difference in someone.

Dina then remembered gripe water as a remedy that had sometimes worked to settle her other two children as babies, so she carried Sarah back upstairs to her bedroom. She placed her on the bed and rummaged through the bathroom cabinet for the gripe water. Her eyes burned as she scanned the label for the appropriate dose.

She remembered that the syringe was back in Sydney's room. She retrieved it from Sydney's dresser, a cat on the prowl. The thought of walking back down to the kitchen made her lightheaded; instead, she washed the syringe in the bathroom sink with hand soap while Sarah howled.

When she placed the syringe to Sarah's lips, she batted it away. It fell out of Dina's grip and landed on the baby's chest.

Dina picked it back up and held Sarah's arms down. Her cries grew an octave higher at being restrained. She pressed the syringe into the corner of the baby's mouth and watched as Sarah swallowed some of the liquid while some of it dribbled down her chin and under the folds of her neck. Dina spread out the receiving blanket and swaddled the baby tightly. She gathered her in her arms and set to rocking her again. She put the soother in the baby's mouth and held it there, giving Sarah no choice but to suck. She kept trying to fight it, but Dina held firm. Sarah's little mouth made moaning sounds as she sucked. Dina watched as the baby's eyes started to flutter. She'd tired herself out.

Dina stared at the ceiling and started counting. She wasn't sure what she was counting for this time or how high she might go, but the steady rhythm of the numbers worked again to distract her as her arms ached and trembled underneath the baby's body. *Ten, eleven, twelve.* The baby sighed. Her eyes were closed, and her mouth relaxed. *Twenty, twenty-one, twenty-two.* The soother hung from the corner of her mouth. *Thirty-three, thirty-four, thirty-five.* Dina felt her shoulders lower with each number. It reminded her of the time Austin was teething, and she'd rocked him for hours as he screamed. James had come through the door from work and found them both crying. As soon as he took the baby from her arms, Austin had stopped crying. Dina had cried harder.

"You may have gotten too tense," James had said. "The baby senses that."

She thought of James, how he still wasn't home. Would Sarah stop crying as soon as he held her? She pictured him at a pub, his tie loosened, his suit jacket carefully draped over his chair. She could hear his throaty laugh, see the flash of his white teeth through his open mouth. Perhaps he'd tipped the pretty young waitress extra. She stood in her yellowed nursing bra, her skin sticky and foul-smelling. She felt like she'd been wrung out. She wasn't sure what she'd do when James got home.

"Moommmmyyy!" A call for help before the familiar retch. Sydney had thrown up again. Dina stood over the baby's crib and held her breath. She set Sarah down gingerly, careful not to jostle her any more than necessary. As soon as her head touched the flannel, her eyes flew open. She wailed instantly. Dina fumbled for the soother that had fallen into the crook of her arm and pushed it inside the baby's mouth, but Sarah kicked and flailed until she was free from the blanket that bound her.

Dina dropped to the floor. She sat, numb, as she listened to her children cry around her. She looked along the hallway at the family photo on the wall and blinked. She thought about putting her coat and shoes on and walking out the door and down the street. She'd simply shut the front door knowing the kids were in their beds and walk. Perhaps she'd walk right out of the city. Maybe find a farmer's field, canola perhaps—she'd always liked the colour of the canola fields—and settle herself within the cover of the stalks. She pictured curling up like a baby herself, the fruit flies, the mice, the crows, and perhaps finally the coyotes, feasting on morsels of her bit by bit until she was hollowed. All that would remain was her bones—the only solid thing left of her.

Dina could not muster the energy to get back on her feet, and she wasn't sure her back would let her anyhow, so she crawled over to Sydney's room. Her darling girl was sitting in her bed, her nightgown and lovely bedding soiled.

"Mommy, why are you crawling?" Sydney asked, puzzled.

Dina couldn't answer. She saw the mess around Sydney and wept. It started as a whimper but grew to a wail and Sydney started crying again too. Her small lips trembled as she watched her mother rock herself back and forth instead of coming to her.

Austin entered the room and observed the scene. He stepped around Dina and got a clean nightgown from Sydney's dresser. She put her arms up for him and he lifted the wet nightgown off her and replaced it. He tried to peel back her covers, a game of tug-of-war for his small frame. He settled on dragging the top comforter, now soiled with vomit, onto the carpet. He got a clean blanket from the linen closet in the hallway and draped it over his sister. She gripped the edge of the blanket and settled back into her bed, her eyes wide.

Dina could see it all happening, but she could not respond. Instead, she crawled back toward her bedroom. She pulled herself up on shaky legs just enough to allow her into bed. Her back wrenched with the effort. Sarah's cries were piercing. Dina's body tensed with each rhythmic wail. She tried to focus on the ceiling again. She started to count.

One, two, three... fourteen, fifteen, sixteen... thirty, thirty-one, thirty-two... the baby was still crying. This time, the counting took her further from herself. Dina sat herself up. She looked at Sarah's writhing figure through the bars of the crib. She went over everything again in her head that she could think to do to soothe her baby and realized she'd tried everything.

She stood and walked over to the crib. She stared down at the baby; her face was contorted and crimson. Dina wrapped her fingers around the baby's upper arms and torso and yanked her up until they were face to face. The baby screamed louder at having her arms pinned to her sides.

"WHAT IS IT?!" she shrieked. "WHAT IS WRONG?!" Adrenaline coursed through her entire body and made her tremble. Her arms felt like lightning rods. Her fingers curled around the baby's frame like vise grips. Sarah remained suspended in the air. She let out a shrill wail, an octave higher than before. Dina's head throbbed. Her grip intensified.

There was nothing left to say, nothing she could do. Dina squeezed her eyes shut. If she could just make the crying stop.

"I DON'T KNOW HOW TO HELP YOU!"

"Mommy?!" First, Austin's voice, then a cool touch on her hip. His hand on her.

Dina blinked. She loosened her grip. She was unsteady, dizzy. Slowly, the room came back into focus. Sarah looked back at her, wide-eyed. Dina set the baby down and placed the receiving blanket over her. Sarah let out a series of small whimpers, but finally, she had stopped crying.

"It's okay, Mommy," Austin said. He rubbed her back with his hand, but Dina could see the pool of tears about to spill from his eyes. What was she doing?

Dina stepped back and sat on the edge of her bed. Her arms vibrated. She stared at the ceiling again and found herself counting out loud. *One, two, three... twelve, thirteen, fourteen... forty-one, forty-two, forty-three.*

"Daddy!" She heard Austin say. Then James stood over her, apologizing for having been late. Something about Lonny ordering another round so they could discuss an account he'd been working on. James' words sounded garbled to her, like he was talking underwater at her. He bent down to kiss her and as soon as she smelled the warm remnants of his Givenchy Pi, she started to weep. She wanted to pull him down onto her, have him crush her with the weight of him so that she could feel the comfort of his chest against hers. She knew he'd walk around and see the carnage of the night and clean up the mess she'd left behind. He was good like that. He always did.

She listened as he herded Austin back to bed and opened the linen closet, likely for clean bedding for Sydney. All the crying had stopped.

When James came back through the doorway to their room, her eyes followed him. He stopped at the crib to check on the baby.

"She's asleep."

Dina felt her stomach drop. The way she'd held Sarah up, ready to shake her, how she'd almost done the unthinkable. How Austin had borne witness. Terror crawled up from the soles of her feet to the top of her head until she felt swallowed by it. She could feel her limbs shake. She swallowed the bile that had shot up her throat. The room was circling around her. James tossed a nightgown toward her, and she flinched when it hit her.

"Dina, are you listening?" James knelt in front of her. Dina felt his fingertips curl around her biceps, but it was gentle. She gasped and let out a feral cry—the cry of a mother broken. Tears erupted down her cheeks.

James stared at her, his eyes searching her face. "What happened?" His lips trembled as he tried to read her. "Dina?!"

Dina blinked. How could she say? The room was circling around her. She found herself counting through it. It was the only thing her brain would allow.

One, two, three, four...

Acknowledgements

I'm still as awed by being a writer as I was in the early years—if not more so—since it's harder to carve out the time for writing at this stage in my life than it used to be.

The gap between my last book and this one included many journeys: obtaining my MFA in Writing (this short story collection formed the basis of my thesis) from the University of Saskatchewan as a mature student (a thrill I will carry with me forever), working as a Writer in Residence at the Saskatoon Public Library, private mentoring, and teaching communications and creative writing at the post-secondary level. Each post has been a privilege as I help launch the careers of other writers.

I admit that my confidence in my own work and my mental health sometimes wavered over this time because at each step, I wondered what was next for me. Writing in new genres and veering in new directions brings a certain vulnerability. I see myself in those that come to me nervous and starry-eyed ready to share their manuscripts, hoping that the words find resonance.

Isn't that what we all really want in the world—to be heard and understood?

A huge thank you to the countless people who have remained supporters of my writing career throughout the years. How lucky I am to be surrounded with incredible friends and family who are eager to support my endeavours.

To Alexis Marie Chute, editor Fiona Pearson, and Wild Skies Press for the care and attention given to this book. I believe in your mission and the work you are producing.

To Nicki Ault, we started our creative journeys at roughly the same time after meeting as stay-at-home moms. We were confidence boosters and cheerleaders for one another as we stepped out into the creative unknown. You have exemplified grace, class, and bravery this year in ways I can't express. I've always been inspired by you and your fierce and exquisite energy—you are someone we all look up to and want to be like.

To my coworkers at Avenue W: what an incredible staff to work with. People I laugh with, who have come to mean so much to me, and who are so dedicated to what they do and really give far more than they are rewarded or recognized for. You are treasures.

To all my post-secondary students, past and present: thank you for everything you bring to my life. I always look forward to going to class. I love connecting with you through learning and feel so fulfilled by your ideas, discussions, and insights. You make me excited and hopeful for the future.

To Jeanette Lynes, Sheri Benning, Jenna Hunnef, and Leona Theis for your guidance and feedback on this manuscript and all things writing-related. I feel fortunate to have you all as mentors and friends.

To my now adult children: remember that it's never too late to change your path, try something new, or take the leap no matter how scary it might seem. It's always worth it on the other side.

To Ben, you remain a steadfast life partner. We may have been so young when we married, but we knew what we were doing. As we approach empty nesting, our partnership has strengthened even more and become fun in new ways I didn't anticipate.

My hope for you, dear reader, is that you find whatever brings you joy and practice it, no matter how bad you think you might be. It's not the outcome that is important—it's the act of creating itself. Getting lost in our passions is something I believe we need more of in our lives, especially during this tumultuous time in the world. We turn to art and creativity in trying times because it fosters connection, understanding, and gives us hope for the future. We realize that we are not alone. The arts are not luxuries as we are made to believe they are; they are integral to a society and its place in time. Engaging in creativity is an act of reclaiming our humanity and our power. Find what lights you up and make time for it. It matters. I promise.

Kristine Scarrow

Author Bio

Kristine Scarrow is the author of four young adult novels: *Throwaway Girl* (2014), *If This Is Home* (2016), *The 11th Hour* (2018), and *The Gamer's Guide to Getting the Girl* (2019) all published by Dundurn Press. Her fiction has been shortlisted or won numerous awards.

Her short fiction, creative non-fiction, and poetry have appeared in several publications. She has also served as an editor for book-length manuscripts and has served as a mentor through The Writers' Union of Canada and the MFA in Writing program at the University of Saskatchewan, where she also holds an MFA in Writing.

She has worked as a five-year hospital writer-in-residence and has served as writer-in-residence in 2022-2023 for the Saskatoon Public Library. She also teaches creative writing and communication classes at the post-secondary level.

Kristine has spent several years researching the power of creativity and art in our lives, specifically how engaging in the arts can be a therapeutic and enriching experience. With a special interest in writing as a healing art, she offers a safe, gentle approach to writing and wants others to discover how writing can be a useful tool to help heal and grow.

Other Books by
Wild Skies Press

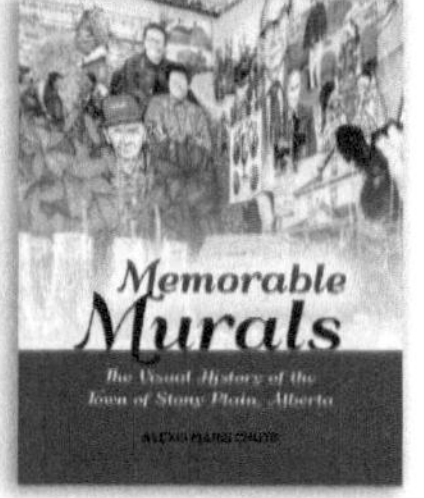

www.WildSkiesPress.com